Xmas 1981

A very happy Xmas to
you dear David
much love
from
Aunt Jill

D0783471

THE
ADVENTUROUS
FOUR

THE
ADVENTUROUS FOUR

by
ENID BLYTON

PRINTED IN **DEAN &** GREAT BRITAIN **SON Ltd.**
52/54 Southwark St. LONDON SE1 1UA
TRADE MARK

603 03287 7
MADE AND PRINTED IN GREAT BRITAIN BY
PURNELL AND SONS LTD., PAULTON (SOMERSET) AND LONDON

CONTENTS

I

THE BEGINNING OF THE ADVENTURES

Three children ran down a rocky path to the seashore. Tom went first, a small, wiry boy of twelve, his red hair gleaming in the sun. He looked round at the two girls following, and his green eyes twinkled.

"Want any help, you two?"

Mary and Jill laughed in scorn.

"Don't be so silly, Tom," said Mary. "We're as good as you any day when we're running over the rocks."

The girls were twins, and very like each other, with their heads of thick golden hair, tied in plaits, and their deep blue eyes. They often laughed at their brother Tom, and said he should have been called Carrots or Ginger or Marmalade, because of his red hair.

They were all on holiday, staying in a little fishing-village on the north-east coast of Scotland. Their father was in the Air Force, and their mother was with them, knitting hard all day long in the garden of the little white house where they were staying.

The three of them had run wild, and were all burnt as brown as monkeys. Usually they wore nothing but bathing costumes and rubber shoes, and spent as much of their time in the sea as out of it.

At first their mother had been afraid of the big waves that crashed on the shore, for she had thought the three children would surely be thrown on to the sand and hurt, if they tried to bathe in such a rough sea. But they had soon learnt to swim right through the heart of the big breaking waves, and reach the calmer water beyond the shore.

They had one great friend—Andy, the fisher-boy. He was a big, strong lad of fourteen, who had just left school and was helping his father with his fishing. Andy was dark-haired and blue-eyed, and was burnt dark brown by the sun. He knew everything about the sea, boats, and fishing. He could mimic any sea-bird, and could call the wild gulls to him by crying to them.

"Andy's marvellous," said Mary and Jill, a dozen times a day—and Tom agreed. Each day the children went to talk to their friend, and to watch him bring in the catch of fish, clean it, and pack it to be sent away.

Andy was tall and brown. He was dressed in old blue trousers, and a dark-blue jersey. He liked the three children very much, and often took them out in his little boat. He had taught them all to swim like fishes, to row strongly, and to climb the rocky cliffs like cats. It would really have turned their mother's hair quite white if she had seen the things that the three children sometimes tried to do!

Andy sat on the side of his little boat and grinned at the three children running down the rocky path. His white teeth gleamed in his brown face, and his eyes shone as blue as the sea. He was mending a net.

"Let me help you, Andy," said Mary, and she took up the torn net. Her fingers were nimble and she worked with Andy whilst the others lay on their backs on the hot sand.

"Andy, did you ask your father what we wanted you to do?" said Tom.

"Aye, I did," said Andy. "He says, yes—if I work hard all the week."

"Andy! How lovely!" said Jill in excitement. "I never thought he'd let you!"

"Do you mean to say your father will really lend you his sailing-ship to take us for a trip to Little Island?" asked Mary, hardly believing her ears. "I never thought he'd say yes."

"I was rather surprised, too," said Andy. "But he

knows I can handle the boat just as well as he can. We'll take plenty of food with us, and we'll sail out to Little Island on Friday. We can spend two days and a night there, my father says — and I'll show you where some queer birds nest — and the cove with yellow stones — and the cliff where about a million birds sit and call."

"Oh, won't it be gorgeous!" said Tom, sitting up and hugging his knees. "All by ourselves. No grown-ups. A little island, far away over there to the east — and no one on it but ourselves! Too good to be true."

In great excitement the children made their plans. "Let's take plenty of food," said Tom, who was always hungry. "I don't know why, but when I'm out on the sea I feel I could eat all the time."

"So do I," said Mary. "It's awful. I've never felt so hungry in my life as I have since we came here."

"Well, we'll get heaps of food," said Tom. "And I'll bring my field-glasses, so that we can see the birds well."

"And you'll bring warm clothes and rugs with you," said Andy.

"Oh, Andy! We shan't need those, surely!" said Jill. "This September is just about the hottest I've ever known."

"It will break soon," said Andy. "And if it happens to turn cold whilst we're in the boat, you'll not like it."

"All right," said Tom. "We'll bring anything, so long as we can go. I say — what about the old gramophone? Music sounds lovely on the water."

Andy was fond of music, so he nodded.

The boat was quite a big one, and even had a little cabin to sit in, with a tiny table and stool, a bench and bunk. Nobody could stand in it, but that didn't matter. The three children had often crowded into it together, whilst Andy sailed the ship around the bay.

They had always longed to visit the island that Andy had told them about—an island of birds, a queer rocky place with a strange cove where most of the stones were yellow. But it was so far from the coast that it had not been possible to visit it in a day.

And now they had permission to go off in the sailing-boat belonging to Andy's father, and spend the night on the island! It would be the greatest adventure of their lives.

On Thursday, the three children tired themselves out taking food, rugs, and other things down to the boat. Andy stared in astonishment at the amount of food.

"Are you wanting to feed an army?" he asked. "Six tins of soup—six tins of fruit—tins of tongue—chocolate—Nestlé's milk—biscuits—cocoa—sugar—and whatever's this?"

"Oh—that's tinned sausages," said Tom, going rather red. "Old Mrs. MacPherson at the village shop said they were awfully good—so I bought some. Think of cooking sausages in a tin on the Little Island, Andy."

"Tom's mad on sausages," said Jill. "He'd like them for breakfast, dinner, and tea. Look—will these rugs be enough, Andy?"

"Yes," said Andy, looking at the odd collection of old rugs that Jill had managed to get together. "Now mind you all wear warm clothes, too—skirts and jerseys, you girls—and shorts and jersey for you, Tom. You haven't got trousers, have you?"

"No," said Tom sadly. "I don't suppose your father would lend me a pair, would he, Andy?"

"He's only got the one pair, and his Sunday ones," said Andy. "And I've only got the ones I'm wearing.

Now are you going to bring the gramophone? We can put it safely in the cabin, if you like."

Tom went back to get it, and soon brought it down to the boat, with a packet of records. He also brought a tin of toffee and a camera.

"I'd like to take some pictures of the birds," he said. "We've got a bird-club at our school, and I guess I could take back some photographs that would beat everyone else's. Golly! Aren't we going to have a fine time!"

"What time do we start, Andy?" asked Jill, looking with pride at the sturdy little fishing-boat that was going to take them on their adventure. Its brown sail was now furled—but to-morrow it would fly in the breeze, and drive the boat over the blue-green sea for miles.

"Be down here at half-past six," said Andy. "I reckon we'll be at the island by about three in the afternoon then."

The three children could hardly sleep that night. Mary and Jill kept calling out to Tom, and at last their mother came up to them, very angry.

"Now, if I hear one more shout, I shall forbid you to go to-morrow," she said. "You will have to be up at six o'clock—and it's nearly half-past ten now. Go to sleep."

The children were so afraid that their mother really would forbid them to go that they said not a word more. They turned on their sides and fell asleep.

At six o'clock all three were dressing hurriedly. It was a magnificent day. The eastern sky was glowing red at dawn, and was now pink and gold. The sun was already warm on their faces as they looked out of the little cottage window.

Their mother was awake. The children kissed her

good-bye and ran down the rocky path to the beach. Andy was already there—but to the children's surprise he looked rather grave.

"I'm thinking we shouldn't go," he said, as soon as he saw the children.

"Andy! Whatever do you mean?" they cried.

"Maybe you didn't see the sky this morning?" said Andy. "It was as red as the geranium in our window. It was a right queer sky—and I'm thinking a storm will blow up to-day or to-morrow."

"Oh, don't be such a spoil-sport, Andy," said Tom, climbing into the boat. "What does a storm matter? We'll be on the island before it comes—and if one comes to-morrow we can wait another day on the island. We've plenty of food."

"If my father hadn't gone out in my uncle's ship to fish, I think he'd be stopping us from going," said Andy doubtfully. "But maybe the storm will blow off to the east. Get in, then. I'm glad to see you've got your jerseys on. If the wind blows up, we'll be cold tonight."

"I've got my bathing-suit on underneath," said Jill. "So have the others. Come on, Andy—push off. I'm simply longing to go!"

Andy pushed off. The boat grated over the stones, and then rode into the waves. Andy jumped in lightly. He and Tom took the oars. They did not mean to put up the sail till they came out of the bay into the full sea.

It was a marvellous morning. The sea was full of sparkles and twinkles—it was blue and purple at a distance, clear green by the boat. Mary let her hand drag in the cool water. She was very happy. Jill was happy too. She lay on her back in the boat, looking up at the cornflower-blue sky, feeling the boat bobbing up and down on the waves, and thinking she would love to stay like this for ever.

Tom was happy too. He loved to pull at the oars. He enjoyed thinking of his breakfast, and planned what he would have.

Only Andy was not happy. He felt in his bones that he should not have taken the children out that morning. He felt sure this was not going to be the wonderful day they had planned. He wished his father had been there to advise him and he anxiously watched the sky for clouds. But there was not one to be seen.

"Now we're really off on our adventure," said Jill. "Really off!"

But she didn't know what an extraordinary adventure it was going to be!

II

LOST IN THE STORM

As soon as the boat was clear of the bay Andy put up the sail. It was a pretty brown one, like the sails of all the other fishing-boats of the village. It billowed out in the breeze, and the boat sped along. The boys shipped the oars.

"I'll steer," said Tom, and he took the tiller. The sail flapped, and spray flew up from under the bows of the boat. It was lovely.

"We go north-east," said Andy. "Can you steer by the sun, Tom?"

"Of course," said Tom, who had learnt to tell the time almost to the half-hour by looking to see exactly where the sun was. "I'm going right, aren't I, Andy? And I make it about half-past seven by the sun."

"It's twenty-past seven," said Jill, looking at her watch. She whispered something to Mary, who giggled.

"What are you giggling at?" asked Tom.

"Tell you in a minute," said Jill. The boat flew on over the green water, and the spray whipped off the sea, and fell cool and silvery on the children.

"Golly!" said Tom, in half a minute. "I *am* hungry. What time are we going to have breakfast?"

The twins burst into squeals of laughter. "That's what we whispered about just now!" said Jill. "I said to Mary 'I guess the next thing Tom says will be that he's hungry and what about breakfast'. And sure enough you did."

Tom laughed. "Well, I guess you feel the same," he

15

said. "Go on down into the little cabin and see what you can get for our breakfast. Andy and I are busy."

The girls went into the tiny cabin, which was crammed full of their food and other belongings. "What shall we have for breakfast?" said Jill. "What about pineapple chunks — and these hard-boiled eggs Mrs. Andrews did for us yesterday evening — and some Nestlé's milk — and chocolate?"

It was a most peculiar breakfast, but the four children thought it was lovely. They had three loaves of bread with them, and some butter, and they dabbed the butter on to chunks of bread, took the eggs in their hand and bit first at the egg and then at the bread. Jill put a paper of salt down on the deck for them to dip the eggs into.

"Fathead!" said Tom, as the wind promptly blew away paper, salt, and all. "As if the sea isn't salt enough already without adding more salt to it! Is there any more?"

There was some in a tin, and as this didn't blow away the children had plenty. There was fresh water in a barrel, and every one dipped in a cup and had a drink.

"That *was* a fine breakfast," said Tom. "I could do with it all over again."

"I'm going to take off my jersey and skirt," said Jill. "I'm simply cooking!"

"So am I," said Mary. The boys felt hot too, for the sun was now pouring down fiercely. Tom took off his jersey, but Andy didn't remove his. He always kept his on, whatever the weather was.

"This is simply gorgeous," said Jill, lying on a rug on the deck, feeling the spray splash on her hot face and arms every now and again. "How I do love to feel the boat bobbing up and down, up and down all the time! Can I have a turn at the tiller soon, Tom?"

"Everybody can," said Tom. "It's a grand feeling to sit here and guide the flying boat. How the wind is getting up! The sail is billowing out like the wings of a bird."

The sailing-boat simply flew over the water. "We shall be at Little Island before three o'clock if we go on like this," said Andy.

"I'm so hot in the sun," said Jill. She was sheltered where she lay, and felt hardly any wind. "I wish I could be dragged behind the boat on a rope, in the cool water."

The morning slid on. The sun rose higher and higher and at noon it was so hot that every one put on sun-hats. The wind was still strong and whipped the tops from the waves as the boat flew along.

"It's past noon," said Tom. "What about . . ."

"A spot of lunch!" chanted every one, knowing exactly what Tom was going to say.

"I'm more thirsty than hungry," said Jill. "What are you looking worried about, Andy?"

"Queer colour the sky is getting over yonder," said Andy, nodding his head to the west.

They all looked. "It's sort of coppery," said Tom.

"There's a storm blowing up," said Andy, sniffing the air like a dog. "I can smell it."

Andy always said he could smell a storm, and he was always right. The children looked anxiously towards the west. "Shall we get to the island before it comes?" asked Jill. "A storm is all very well to read about in a book—but I don't really want to be in one out on the open sea."

"We'll do our best," said Andy. "The little boat can't go faster than she's going now. As it is the sail is almost splitting with the wind!"

The sea turned a strange colour, a kind of blue-brown. "It's caused by the reflection of that funny sky," said Jill, half nervous. "I say! It's queer being out here on the sea, miles away from land, with the sea and the sky doing odd things like this."

Then an even stranger thing happened. The wind, which had been blowing very strongly indeed, dropped completely. One moment it was blowing the children's hair straight back, as they faced the west—the next there was not a breath of air. The sea fell calm and oily. The little fishing-boat stopped running in front of the wind, and rode silently over the waves, as if she were at anchor.

"I say! That's funny," said Tom. "Not a bit of breeze now! Andy, we'll never get to the island if we don't get some wind. Shall we row?"

"No," said Andy, his face rather pale under its dark brown. "No, Tom. You'll get plenty of wind in a minute —more than we want. We must take in some of the sail. The ship will heel right over if we let her have all this sail when next the wind gets up. There's going to be a gale. I can hear it coming."

There was a queer humming noise in the air that seemed to come from nowhere at all. Then an enormous purple cloud blew up from the west and completely covered the sun. The world went dark, and great spots of rain fell.

"It's coming now," said Andy. "Help me with the sail, Tom. Take the tiller, Jill. Keep her heading the way we've been going. Pull, Tom, pull."

They pulled at the big brown sail—but before they had done what they wanted to the storm broke. A great crash of thunder came from the black cloud, and a flash of lightning split the sky in half.

And then the gale came. Tom and the girls had never, never imagined there could be such a wind. They could not hear themselves speak unless they shouted. Andy yelled to the girls:

"Get down into the cabin, quick, and shut the door and stay there."

"Oh, let's be here," cried Jill. But Andy looked so stern and commanding that they did not dare to disobey. They almost fell into the cabin and shut the door. Outside the wind seemed to get a voice—a voice that howled and wailed and lashed the sea into enormous waves that

sent the little boat half-over every time. Tins and every-thing else began to fall about. The girls picked them up and put them where they could not fall.

There was a crash as the packet of records fell down. "Blow!" cried Jill. "They'll all be broken!"

So they were—all but one. It was very sad. The girls carefully put the one whole record into a safe place and wondered what the boys would say when they knew. But it couldn't be helped.

Up above, on the deck, the two boys struggled with the wind and the sea. Tom wished he had an extra jersey and he shivered as wave after wave splashed on him, and the wind whipped by.

The deck was wet and slippery. The dark-green waves raced by, and the boat climbed up one steep wave after another, and slid down the other side, only to climb up another enormous wave again.

Up and down, up and down she went, whilst Andy struggled with the sail.

"What are you trying to do?" yelled Tom, who was at the tiller.

"Take in all the sail," shouted back Andy. "We can't go on like this. We'll be over."

But he didn't need to bother—for suddenly the sail ripped itself off the mast, flapped wildly for a second and then sped away into the sky. It was gone! Only a little rag was left, wriggling madly in the wind. The boat slowed down at once, for it no longer had the sail to take it along. But even the little rag of sail that was left was enough to take it at a good speed over the waves.

Andy said nothing. He took the tiller with Tom, and together the boys faced the storm. Thunder rolled around and crashed in the skies. Lightning flickered and lighted up the vast heaving waste of grey-black sea. Stinging rain fell every now and again, and the boys bent their heads to it and shut their eyes. The wind lashed them and the spray whipped them. If this was an adventure, there was a great deal too much of it!

"Do you think we're all right, Andy?" shouted Tom. "Are we near the island?"

"I reckon we've passed it!" yelled back Andy. "At the rate we've been going we'd have been there by now. Goodness knows where we are!"

Tom stared at Andy in silence. Passed the island! A storm behind them! No sail! Whatever were they going to do?

III

SHIPWRECK!

For a long time the boat went on and on, its little rag of sail still flapping. Tom thought that the sail itself must have reached the great dark cloud that still covered the sky, the wind was so strong.

"I should think this wind's almost a hurricane, isn't it?" yelled Tom.

"Pretty near," shouted Andy. "But it's blowing itself out now."

Sure enough it was. Every now and again there was a lull when the wind dropped to a stiff breeze. Then it would blow again furiously. The thunder was no longer overhead, but far off to the east. The lightning shimmered now and again, but did not light up the sea with the fierce brilliance it had two or three hours back.

Then, just as suddenly as it had come, the storm flew off. It was most astonishing. A sheet of bright blue sky appeared in the west, and swiftly grew bigger as the great cloud flew to the east. The world grew light again. The rain stopped. The wind died down to a breeze, and the boat no longer seemed to climb up and down steep hills.

The cabin door opened, and two green faces looked out sadly. "We've been awfully sea-sick down here," said Jill. "It was dreadful."

"What a frightful storm!" said Mary. "Are we nearly at the island?"

"We've passed it, Andy says," said Tom gloomily.

22

"We don't know where we are."

"Goodness! Look, the sail's gone!" said Mary, shocked. "What *are* we to do for a sail?"

"There's an old one down in the cabin," said Andy. "Fetch it, will you—and I'll see if I can do something with it."

The sun shone down again. It was gloriously hot. Poor Tom, who had been chilled to the bone, loved it. He stripped off his wet bathing-suit, and put on his jersey. Ah, that was better!

Andy did not seem to feel either cold or wet. He took the old sail and had a good look at it. He thought he could rig it, with Tom's help. They must have a sail of some sort to get anywhere.

"I've heard my father say there are some desolate, rocky islands up away to the north of Little Island," said Andy, his wet jersey steaming in the hot sunshine. "We'll make for those. Maybe there might be someone there—or we could signal a ship for help. I don't reckon we're going to get home any too easily now."

At last the old sail was flying in the breeze. Andy headed due north. It was about five o'clock now, and all the children were very hungry.

Jill and Mary had forgotten their sea-sickness and went below to get some food. Soon they were all eating heartily, and felt much better. They drank all the water before Andy knew there was none left.

"We shouldn't have done that," he said. "If we don't strike these islands I'm thinking of, we'll have no water to-morrow. Leave those apples, Mary. We might be glad of the juice in the morning."

Mary had been about to bite into a juicy apple, but she hastily put it down. In silence she and Jill packed the apples away carefully in the cabin. Both the girls felt worried. Whatever would their mother be thinking, when that terrible storm blew up? They wished they were safely back at home.

The boat sailed on to the north. The sun slipped low into the west, and the boat's shadow lay purple on the sea. It was a beautiful evening.

"Look! Gulls!" said Andy, at last. "Maybe we are nearing land. Can't see any, though. We'd better anchor for the night, I should think."

And then the children got a great shock. There was no anchor! Andy stared in horror. How could he possibly have forgotten that his father had warned him to take the old anchor because he was lending Andy's uncle his own? How *could* he have forgotten? Now they couldn't anchor their ship. Now they would have to ride on the sea until they came to land—and in the night they might strike a rock!

Andy stared over the restless sea in dismay. Well—there was nothing for it but to hope for the best. One of them must be at the helm all night long. It would be a moonlight night if only the sky was not clouded. Perhaps they would be lucky and sight land.

Jill and Mary were tired out. Andy ordered them to go below and rest. "You'd better go too, Tom," he said. "You'll have to come up and take your turn on deck tonight, and you'd better get a nap whilst you can."

"But I don't want to," said Tom. "I shall be able to keep awake all right."

"Go below, Tom," said Andy, in the kind of voice that had to be obeyed. Tom went into the little cabin with the girls. They left the door open, for it was warm. The girls lay on the bunk and Tom curled up on the pile of rugs on the floor. In two minutes he was asleep. He did not know how tired he was. The wind, rain and sea had taken all his strength out of him for a time.

Andy stayed alone on deck. The sun had gone down in a blaze of gold. The sky had turned pink and the sea had turned pink too. Now it was evening and the first stars were winking in the darkening sky.

The little boat drove on and on. Andy hoped desperately that land would soon come in sight. He remembered so clearly what his father had said. Right past the Little Island, far to the north, lay other islands, desolate now, but once owned by a few farmers, who tried to get a hard living from the rocky soil. If only they could get help there!

Night fell darkly on the waters. The moon sailed into the sky, but clouds kept hiding her light. First the sea was gleaming silver, then it was black, then it was silver again. Andy wished he could see something besides the sea. But there was nothing.

The boy stayed on deck until midnight. He felt the night wind and wrapped a rug round his shoulders, though he did not feel really cold. After a while he whistled to Tom.

Tom awoke. "Coming," he said sleepily, and went up on deck. He shivered and Andy threw the rug round him. "Keep her heading straight," he said. "Give me a call if you see anything."

It was queer up on deck all alone. The old sail flapped and creaked a little. The water went plash-lash-lash against the sides of the boat. The moon sailed in and out of the clouds as if she were a silver boat in the sky.

Then came a thick mass of clouds and the moon disappeared altogether. Tom couldn't see anything at all.

He strained his eyes to try and pierce through the darkness but except for the gleaming white top of a nearby wave now and then, he could see nothing.

But he could hear something, quite suddenly. It sounded like crashing waves. Tom longed for the moon to come out — and as he wished for it, it came sliding out from a cloud for a second before it disappeared again.

And in that tiny space of time Tom saw something that gave him a shock. The sea was breaking over big rocks just ahead!

"Andy! Andy!" yelled Tom, wrenching the tiller round. "Rocks ahead!"

Andy came tumbling up the steps, wide awake at once. He heard the sound of breaking waves and knew at once there were rocks ahead. He took the tiller.

And then there came a grating noise and a long groan from the ship. She was on the rocks! She had run straight on to them — and there she lay, groaning, half over, slanting so much that the girls in the little cabin were thrown out of the bunk.

"Hold on, Tom," shouted Andy, clutching at Tom, who seemed about to slide overboard. "Hold on! She's settling!"

The ship did settle. She seemed to be wedged between two rocks that were holding her tightly, all on the slant. Waves splashed over one side of her deck.

For a few minutes the children hardly dared to breathe — and then Andy spoke.

"She's fast," he said. "She may have a hole in her bottom, but she won't sink while she's held like this. We must wait till dawn."

So they waited, clinging uncomfortably to the slanting sides of the ship. Dawn was not far off. It silvered the

26

eastern sky as they waited. The light grew stronger, and then a gold edge appeared on the horizon. The sun was about to rise.

And in the golden light of the early sun they saw something not far off that made them shout for joy.

"Land ho!" they yelled, and would have danced in delight if only the deck had not been so slanting. And land ho there certainly was!

A sandy shore stretched to a rocky cliff. Stunted trees grew further inland, touched with gold by the rising sun. It was an island of some sort, desolate, rocky and lonely —but it was at least land! Somewhere where they could light a fire and boil water to make themselves warm. Somewhere where other people might be to give them a helping hand.

"We'll have to swim for it," said Andy. "It's not very far. Once we're clear of these rocks we'll be all right. In fact, now that the tide has gone down a bit we could almost walk over the rocks, to the shallow water that runs up the shore."

Andy held out his hand to Mary. Tom helped Jill. Half-wading, half-swimming, they made their way over and between the reef of rocks, and paddled to shore. The sun had warmth in it now and warmed their cold bodies. How glad they all were that they had taken Andy's advice and had put on warm clothes!

"Well," said Andy, when they had reached the shore, "we'll climb up these cliffs, and see if we can spot anyone's house."

They climbed the rocky cliffs. When they got to the top they looked around. A small stunted wood grew a little way off, on a hillside. Low bushes crouched here and there as if to hide from the strong wind that blew

27

always across the island. Grass crept over the rocky earth, and a few daisies flowered. But there was no sign of any house, or of any human being.

Andy made up his mind quickly.

"If we've got to be stranded here for a time we *must* get out of our ship everything that's in her," he said. "Thank goodness we've got a certain amount of food and some rugs. The tide is at its lowest now—when it is high it will completely cover the deck of our boat—so we must wade back to her and take off everything of value in her. Come on, Tom. You girls can stand halfway to the boat in that shallow water, and we'll carry things to you over the rocks. Then you can take them back to the shore. It will be better than us all scrambling about on the rocks and dropping everything."

And so they began to empty the ship of all it held— food, rugs, gramophone, camera, field-glasses, stool, tables, tools, crockery, kettle, matches, little stove, everything! It took a long time—but before they had finished the tide had risen and the decks were awash. The cabin was full of water!

"We can't do anything more," said Andy. "Let's go and have a rest—and something to eat. I'm simply starving."

IV

ON THE UNKNOWN ISLAND

It was a rather solemn set of children who sat down on the shore to eat breakfast. They had been brave during the storm—but now they all felt very tired and rather scared. It was strange to think they might have to stay for quite a long time on the unknown island until they were rescued—and supposing they were right off the route of the ships and steamers that used those seas?

Andy took charge. He was the oldest and wisest, and the others looked up to him. He was old for his fourteen years. He stared out at their wrecked ship, and wrinkled his forehead.

"Well, we're in a nice fix," he said. "But we'll forget it for a minute and enjoy our breakfast. We'd better finish up all the bread, for it will soon be stale. We'll eat all the food that might go bad—there's that open jar of potted meat, Tom, that we began last night—and the rest of the butter—and those buns that Mrs. Andrews gave us. And what about something hot to drink? I don't feel really cold, but it would do us good to get something hot inside us. Look—I brought the matches with me, wrapped in this oilskin so that they wouldn't get wet. We can't get the stove going till we get the tin of oil out of the locker in the boat—we forgot that—so we'd better make a fire on the beach."

Tom and Jill collected sticks, and soon there was a fine fire going. Andy went off up the cliff to see if he could find a stream to fill the kettle, which they had taken from the boat. He had to go a good way before he found a spring running down the little hill in the distance. He filled the kettle and went back to the cove.

"Good — the fire's going well," he said. "I found a spring, so we needn't worry about water. Where's the tin of cocoa — and we must finish up that Nestlé's milk we opened, or it will go bad."

The kettle soon boiled, and the children made thick cocoa. They added the tinned milk to it and drank with enjoyment. The cocoa was good. The twins, who were cold, felt warmed up at once. Their clothes were still wet, and although the sun now shone down hotly they felt chilly.

Tom yawned. He was not used to keeping awake half the night. The girls were tired out, too, for they had been very sea-sick in the storm.

Andy had laid out the rugs in the sun. He felt them. They were almost dry.

"We'd better get off our wet things and hang them on the bushes to dry," he said. "We'll roll ourselves in these rugs, and lie down in the sheltered corner over there by the cliff, in the sun, and sleep off our bad night."

So in three or four minutes all that could be seen of the children were four tightly-rolled bundles lying peacefully asleep in the sunshine, well out of the wind in a cosy corner of the beach. Their damp clothes were spread out on bushes to dry, and were already steaming in the sun.

Andy awoke first. He knew at once where he was, and remembered all that had happened. He sat up to look at their ship. The tide was going down again now, and the ship looked queer, slanting sideways, caught fast between the two big rocks. Andy wondered what his

father would say when he knew what had happened. It was a serious thing to lose a fishing-boat.

The sun was high in the sky. Andy threw off his rug and went to feel his clothes on the bush. They were perfectly dry. He put them on, and then went to the big pile of things they had taken from the ship. He looked among them and found a fishing-line.

He hunted about for a sandworm, baited his hook, and clambered out on the rocks, where deep water swirled around him. He lowered his line into the water. In ten minutes he had caught his first fish, and was baiting the line again.

Tom awoke next. He sat up on the sand, astonished

31

to hear the sea so close. Then he remembered all that had happened and leapt to his feet. He awoke the girls and they put on their warm clothes. They saw Andy, and waved to him.

"Andy's getting our dinner!" said Jill. "I suppose you're feeling as hungry as usual, Tom?"

"I could eat a whale!" said Tom, and he really felt as if he could.

It was fun cooking the fish over a fire. It smelt delicious. There was no bread left so the children had to eat the fish by itself, but they were so hungry that they didn't mind at all.

"It's about two o'clock in the afternoon," said Andy, looking at the sun. "Now the first thing to do is to find a good place to sleep for the night. Then we'd better explore the island, if we've time. The food we've got with us won't last a great while, but at any rate we can always get fish—and I expect we'll find some berries we can eat, too."

"Look!" said Tom, suddenly pointing to the pile of things not far off. "There's a gull there. Will he peck our tins open—or eat our cocoa!"

Andy clapped his hands and the gull flew off, crying loudly. "We certainly mustn't leave any food out," said Andy. "The gulls would have it at once. Look—there's two or three fishes left we can have for our supper. We'd better make a hole in the sand and bury them under some heavy stones till we want them. The gulls would soon make a meal of them if we left them uncovered!"

They buried the fish. Andy stood up and looked all round the cliff.

"I wonder if there's a cave we could sleep in at night," he said. But there didn't seem to be any cave at all,

32

though the children hunted carefully all along the cliff.

"How will anyone know we are here?" asked Jill. "We shall have to put up some sort of a sign, shan't we, to show any passing ship or steamer that we are here?"

"Yes," said Andy. "I've been thinking about that. I'll take down the ship's sail, and we'll tie it to a tree on the top of the cliff. That will be a fine signal."

"Good idea!" said Tom. "It will flap in the wind and be seen for miles."

"We'll find a sleeping-place for the night before we do that," said Andy. "It looks like rain again now—see that low cloud over there? We don't want to be soaked in our sleep. Come on."

They left the sandy cove and climbed up the steep cliff. It was hard going, but they got to the top at last, and once more looked across the island. They could not see right across it because the hill in the middle stopped their view—so they did not know how big or small it was. All they knew was that, at present, they could not see any sign of anyone else there or of any house or other building.

"How I'd love to see a cow or two!" said Jill.

"Whatever for?" said Mary in surprise. "I didn't know you liked cows so much, Jill."

"I don't," said Jill. "But cows would mean a farmer, silly—and a farmer means a farmhouse—and a farmhouse means lots of people, and help, of course!"

The others laughed. "Well, let's hope we see one or two cows for you, Jill," said Tom. "Which way shall we go, Andy?"

"We'll make our way to the hill," said Andy. "There's bracken there, and heather, and maybe we can find a hill-cave to snuggle in. Bracken and heather make a fine bed, and we've got the rugs for covers."

They ran to the hill. It had a little wood of wind-blown pines and birches, but there was no cave in the hillside they could shelter in. It was covered with thick-growing bracken and heather, with a few stunted gorse bushes—but there was no place that would really give them a safe shelter to sleep.

"Well, we'll have to rig up a tent of some sort," said Andy at last. "I'm not going to be soaked through tonight. I've had enough of that to last me for quite a while."

"A tent, Andy!" said Tom. "Wherever would we get a tent from? Buy it from a shop, I suppose?"

"I'm going to get the old sail off the boat," said Andy. "We can use it for a signal by day and a tent by night. "It's big enough to cover us all quite well."

"Andy, you *have* got good ideas!" said Jill. "I should never have thought of that. Well, shall we go back then and help you?"

"No," said Andy. "You stay here with Tom and help him to build a kind of tent-house that we can just drape the sail over. You'll want some stout branches, stuck well into the ground. I'll go and get the sail."

Andy went off down to the shore again, and clambered and waded out to the boat. He was soon taking down the old sail.

The others hunted for good branches. The ones lying on the ground were too brittle and old, they found.

"They'll make good firewood," said Tom. "We'll have to break a few growing branches off the trees."

It was difficult to do this, but they managed it at last. Then they drove the stout sticks into the heathery ground and made a kind of circle with them, big enough to hold them all.

They had just finished when Andy came back, bent double under the heavy sail. He threw it down and panted.

"I thought I'd never get it up the cliff," he said. "I say, you've made a fine set of walls. The sail will go over them nicely."

Eight willing hands helped to arrange the big brown sail over the circle of sticks stuck firmly into the ground. The weight of the sail kept it down, and when the children had finished, they had made a kind of round, brown tent, with no doorway. But as the children could get in anywhere under the tent simply by lifting up the sail, it didn't matter having no doorway.

"We'll gather a nice pile of heather and put it inside the tent to lie on," said Tom. "And with our rugs, too, we shall be as cosy and warm as toast! In fact, we may be much too hot!"

"Well, if we are, we'll just lift up one side of the tent and let the breeze blow in," said Jill. "Oh, I do feel excited! I really feel as if we've got a sort of little home, now we've made this tent!"

"There isn't time to explore the island now," said Andy, looking in surprise at the sinking sun. "We've taken ages over the tent. We'll go all over the island to-morrow."

"That *will* be fun," said Mary. "I do wonder what we'll find!"

V

MAKING THE BEST OF THINGS

The children were all hungry again. Andy thought it would be better to bring everything up from the shore, and put it near their tent.

"We may have to make our tent a sort of home," he said. "We don't want to have to keep climbing up and down that rocky cliff every time we want a cup or a kettle! Besides, we are quite near the spring here, and we can easily get water whenever we want to."

So for the next hour or so the children fetched all their belongings. Some of them were very difficult to get up the cliff. The gramophone was almost impossible till Andy thought of the idea of tying a rope round it and hauling it gently up by that.

"Golly! All the records are broken!" said Tom in dismay, as he picked up the cracked records.

"Yes — they fell and broke when that dreadful storm was on," said Jill. "Leave them behind. They're no use. There's just *one* that's not broken — now, where is it?"

They found it at last and looked at it.

"What a pity! This is a silly record — it *would* be the only one that's left unbroken!" said Mary. "On one side it's a girl singing a kind of lullaby, without even any music — and on the other it's nursery rhymes. The silliest one we've got!"

"Oh well — bring it along," said Tom. "And where's my camera? It doesn't look as if I'll find any good pictures to take — but I may as well have it."

By the time they had got everything to the tent they were really very tired. They cooked the rest of the fish and opened a tin of peaches. They ate an apple each, broke a bar of chocolate into four pieces, and then drank some hot cocoa. It was a good meal and they enjoyed it. The sun was now almost gone and the first star was shining brightly.

"Well, we've had an adventurous day," said Jill, yawning. "I slept all the morning—but I feel awfully sleepy again already."

"We'll turn in early," said Andy. "I'm tired too."

"We can't clean our teeth," said Jill, who was always very particular about nails and teeth and things like that. "I wish I had a tooth-brush."

"Well, here's a brush for you," said Tom, with a grin, handing Jill the brush that was used to sweep bits of fish off the deck. "Brush your teeth with this."

Jill took it and at once brushed Tom's hair with it. Tom was disgusted.

"Don't, you cuckoo!" he said. "I shall smell of fish all night long."

"Come on," said Andy. "We want more heather for our beds. Tom, stamp out the fire. We don't want to set the hill alight, and the heather is very dry."

Tom stamped out the fire. The girls filled the tent with more heather. Andy took the largest rug and spread it all over the springy pile.

"You girls can sleep on this side of the tent, and Tom and I will take the other," he said. "There are plenty of rugs, luckily."

Nobody undressed. For one thing they had no nightclothes, and for another they didn't even think of it. Life seemed quite different on an unknown island.

37

Nobody even thought of going to wash—though Tom's hair smelt so much of old fish that Andy threatened to pour a kettle of water over it.

"I'll wash my head under the spring to-morrow morning," said Tom sleepily. "I really can't go now. I'm simply dropping asleep whilst I talk!"

They rolled themselves up in their rugs and lay flat on the heathery bed. It was beautifully soft and springy, and very comfortable once they had pressed down several sharp bits that stuck into them.

Tom was asleep at once. The girls lay awake for a minute or two. Jill felt very hot, for the tent was airless, and the four of them made quite a crowd in it. The roof was not more than arm's length above their heads.

"Andy," said Jill, in a low voice. "I'm *so* hot. Could we get some air in, do you think?"

"Yes," said Andy. He raised one side of the sail and let the breeze in. It was lovely, for now the girls could see out.

The moonlight lay on the hillside and everything was clear till the clouds sailed across the moon. Mary fell asleep as she watched bracken outside waving in the wind. Then Jill fell asleep. Only Andy lay awake, leaning on his elbow, looking out down the hillside, and listening to the sound of the waves in the distance, under the cliff.

He was old enough to feel that this adventure might not turn out at all well. He wondered what would be the best thing to do for them all.

"We must certainly hang out a signal every day," he thought. "It might be seen by some passing ship. We must find a better place to live in too, for if the weather should break up, this tent won't be any use. And I wonder if it's possible to get the ship off the rocks and patch her up. If we could do that, maybe we might have a shot at sailing home."

As he lay worrying about all these things his eyes closed. He was soon dreaming that he had got the boat off the rocks, but it changed into a large steamer that seemed to have hands and was fishing busily in a pool. There was such a strong smell of fish that Andy opened his sleepy eyes again—only to find that Tom's fishy-smelling head was just under his nose. Andy turned over, grinning. "What a silly sort of dream!" he thought —and then, in half a second, he was dreaming again.

All the children slept soundly that night, and even when the clouds piled up over the moon and a sharp downpour of rain came they didn't wake. The raindrops pattered over the tent, but did not soak through to the sleeping children. Some came through the side where Andy had raised the sail to let in the air, but the children felt nothing.

They awoke when the sun was fairly high—about eight o'clock in the morning. Andy as usual awoke first and rolled out of the tent quietly. But he had waked Tom, and when the boy yawned loudly the girls awoke too.

It was a fine sunny morning with clouds scudding across the sky like big pieces of cotton-wool. The first thing, of course, was breakfast—but it had to be caught!

So Andy and Tom went fishing on the rocks and the girls managed to catch about twenty large prawns in a pool on the sandy shore. They cooked their catch and ate hungrily.

"I do feel dirty," said Jill. "I shall go and wash at the spring. Coming, Mary?"

"Yes," said Mary. "And I vote we all have a bathe today. That will clean us up a bit too."

They all felt cleaner after a rinse and splash in the spring. Tom and Andy made the fixing of the signal their next job. They found a good tree—at least, it was a good one for their purpose, for it had been struck by lightning at one time and now stood straight and bare on the top of the cliff.

It took the two boys about an hour to climb the tree and fix the sail-signal. It flapped out well in the breeze and Andy was sure it could be seen from a great distance. They climbed down again and went back to the girls.

"What about exploring the island now?" asked Tom. "I feel just like a good walk!"

"Well, the island may be too small for a good walk!" said Andy. "We'll just see. Ready, you girls?"

They were all ready for their walk. First they climbed the hill and stood on the top, looking to see what they could spy.

From the top of the hill they could see all around their island—and certainly it was not very big—only about a mile and a half long and about a mile wide. They could see the blue water all around it.

But not far off were other islands! They lay in the sea, blue and misty in the distance. But as far as the children could see, there were no houses or buildings of any kind on them. They seemed as desolate and lonely as their own island. The cries of sea-birds came as they stood on the hill, and big white gulls swooped around them—but except for that sound, and the far-off splash of waves, there was no other sound to be heard. No shout —no hoot of a horn—no drone of an aeroplane. They might be lost in the very middle of the ocean for all they could see or hear!

"I don't believe a single soul lives here on these

islands," said Andy, his face rather grave. "Come on—
let's go down to this side of the hill. We may as well find
out all there is to know."

As they went down the hill and came to the level
ground again, Tom stopped in astonishment. "Look!"
he said. "Potato plants!"

The children looked—and sure enough, growing
completely wild around them were plants that looked
exactly like potatoes! Andy pulled one up—and there,
clinging to the roots, were a dozen or more small white
potatoes!

"That's queer!" said Andy, staring round. "At some

41

time or other there must have been people living here
—and they grew potatoes. Some have seeded themselves and grown wild. But the thing is—if people lived
here—*where* did they live? They must have lived
somewhere!"

"How queer," said Tom, looking all round as if he
expected houses to spring from the ground.

And then Jill gave a shout. "I believe I can see the
chimney of a house! Look! Where the ground dips down
suddenly over there."

The others looked. They saw that the ground did
suddenly dip down into a kind of hollow, well protected
from the wind—just the place where people might
build a house. They tore over the rocky ground to the
dip, expecting they hardly knew what.

And what a surprise they got when at last they reached
the hollow and looked down into it!

VI

A QUEER LITTLE HOME

The four children stood at the top of the steep dip. The hollow ran right down to the sea — and in it was a cluster of small buildings!

But what strange buildings! The roofs were off, the chimneys were gone, all but the one they had seen, the walls were fallen in, and everything looked forlorn and deserted.

"Nothing but ruins!" said Tom, in astonishment. "Whatever happened to make the houses and shed fall to pieces like that?"

"I think I know," said Andy. "A year or two ago there came a great storm to these parts — so great that the people of our village fled inshore for miles, because the sea battered our houses and flooded our streets. The storm must have been even worse on these unprotected islands here — and I should think the sea came into this hollow and battered the farm to bits! Look at that chimney-stack there — all black and broken — that was struck by lightning, I should think."

The four children gazed down at the poor, hollow house and out-buildings. A little farm had once been there — a poor farm maybe, trying to grow a few potatoes in the rocky ground, to keep a few goats or cows, and to take from the sea enough fish to live on.

Now the folk had all gone, unable to battle with the great sea-storms that swept over their farm and destroyed their living.

"This explains the potatoes," said Jill. "That stretch of struggling potato plants must once have been a field."

"Let's go down into the hollow and have a look round," said Andy. So down into the dip they scrambled and wandered round the ruined buildings. Nothing had been left—all the furniture had been taken away, and even the gates and doors removed. Seashore weeds grew up from the floors of the farmhouse.

"A boy must have lived here," said Andy, picking up a broken wooden train from a patch of weeds.

"And here's a broken cup," said Jill, bending over what had once been a rubbish-heap.

They wandered about and at last came to a little wooden shack where perhaps a cow or two had been kept in the winter. For some reason it had escaped being beaten in by the waves, and still stood upright, its one window broken, and its floor covered with a creeping weed.

Andy looked at it carefully. "This wouldn't be a bad place to make into a little house for ourselves," he said. "I was thinking we'd have to try and build one somehow —but this will do if we patch it up a bit. The tent won't be any use at all if the weather breaks up—and also it's going to be a great nuisance to keep taking it down from the signal tree each night for our tent and putting it back again in the mornings."

"Oh yes!" said Tom in delight. "Let's make this our house! That would be fun. Then we could leave the sail flapping for our signal all the time."

They all went into the shack. It was not very large— more like a big bicycle shed, though the roof was higher. A wooden partition divided it into two.

"We'll take that down," said Andy. "It would be better to have one fairly big room than two tiny ones."

"Well, we'd better start work at once, hadn't we?" said Tom eagerly. "We shall have to bring all our things here—and make it a bit home-like. And all those weeds will have to be cleared."

"Yes—and we'll spread the floor with clean sand," said Jill. "Listen—you boys clear up the weeds for us —and Mary and I will go to that old potato field and find the biggest potatoes we can, and cook them in their jackets for lunch!"

"Good idea," said Tom, feeling hungry at once. "Come on, Andy—let's start and clean up the place now—we can't do much till that's done."

The two boys set to work. They pulled up the creeping weed by handfuls and piled it outside. They got tufts of stiff heather and, using them as brushes, swept the cobwebs from the walls and rough ceiling. Tom broke the remaining glass of the window, gathered the broken bits carefully together and tucked them into the bottom of the old rubbish-heap so that no one could be cut by a splinter.

Andy made a rough fireplace just outside the shack, with stones from the hearth of the ruined farmhouse.

"We can't have the fire inside because this shack has no chimney," he said, "and we'd be choked with the smoke. Anyway, I've made the fireplace out of the wind and we ought to be able to cook all right on it. Mary, you can bake the potatoes there, once the stones get hot. Tom, get some sticks and start a fire."

Mary and Jill peeped inside the shack. It looked clean and tidy now, though very bare. The two girls had pulled plenty of good potatoes from the old, weedy field, and had washed them in the spring water. They would be fine, baked in their jackets—though it was a pity there was no butter left and no salt.

45

Tom fetched some clean sand from the shore. He had found a very old bucket, which had a hole in the bottom. He put a flat stone over the hole, and then the sand did not trickle out. He carried six pails full of sand to the shack and scattered it over the earth floor. It looked very neat and clean.

"We'll have to get heaps of heather and bracken in for beds again," said Jill, "just as we did for our tent. Won't it be a nice little house! We must bring the little table here, and the stool—and all the cups and things. It will make it seem like home."

The children had quite forgotten how serious their adventure was. It was such fun to work like this and get ready a little house. Mary even began to wonder if there was anything she could use as a curtain for the window!

Their lunch was potatoes and chocolate, with plenty of cold spring water. Tom could have eaten three times as much but he had to be content with five large potatoes and a whole bar of chocolate.

"We'll have fish for tonight," promised Andy. "The water round about this island is just thick with fish. We'll always have plenty to eat so long as we don't get tired of fish! We'll hunt for shell-fish too."

After their dinner the children separated. The girls were to go to the nearest patches of heather and bracken and bring in armfuls for beds. The boys were to make journeys to and from the tent, and bring in all their belongings.

"When the tide's down tonight I'll get the tin of oil out of the locker of the boat," said Andy. "That won't have been spoilt by the sea-water because it's got a tight-fitting lid. We can cook over the stove then, as well as over a fire, if we want to."

The children were very busy that afternoon. Mary and Jill got enough heather and bracken to make two beds, one at each side of the shack. They piled the tough bracken on the floor first, and then the softer heather on top. Then they spread each bed with a rug, and put another rug, neatly folded up, to be used as a blanket at night.

"The beds can be couches to sit on in the daytime," said Mary, quite pleased with the look of them. "We'll have to add more heather day by day, I expect, Jill, because we shall flatten the beds very much with our weight. But we can easily see to that."

The boys brought in the crockery—cups, saucers and plates—thick, common ones used by the fishermen who sailed in Andy's father's boat with him. They were just right for the shack—but where were they to be put?

"We really can't keep them on the floor," said Mary. "They'll get broken. I wish we had a shelf to put things on. It would give us much more room if only we could get these odd things out of the way."

Andy disappeared for a few minutes. When he came back he carried a wooden board. He grinned at the surprised children.

"I remembered seeing an old shelf in what must have been the kitchen of the farmhouse," he said. "So I went in and wrenched it down from the wall. Tom, where did you put the tools and the box of nails?"

"Down there by our bed," said Tom. Andy picked up a hammer and the box of nails. "Where do you want the shelf?" he asked the girls.

"Over there, at the back of the shack, just about shoulder-high," said Mary. "What a lovely shelf that will make, Andy—it will take everything!"

So it did! Once Andy had nailed it up, the girls arranged the crockery there, the kettle, one or two pans, the field-glasses, camera and other things. The gramophone would not go on the shelf so they put it into a corner.

By this time the shack really looked fine! There were the two neat beds at the sides — the table in the middle, with the stool — the neatly-sanded floor — the shelf at the back with its array of goods! The children felt really pleased with it.

Andy filled the oil-stove. "You could *boil* us some potatoes tonight for a change," he said to Mary. "You've got a little saucepan, haven't you?"

"Yes," said Mary. "I'll boil them and mash them for you — but they'll taste a bit odd without butter or salt! And we'll open another tin of fruit."

The boys went off to catch fish. The girls busied themselves with fetching more potatoes, more water, and setting the oil-stove going. They felt very busy and rather important.

They had a most delicious supper and enjoyed every bit of it. They didn't even mind going without salt in the potatoes. They ate their supper sitting outside the open doorway of the shack, looking out to the evening sea. The gulls called high in the air, and the splash of the little white-edged waves came to them every now and again.

"Now we'll turn in!" said Andy with a yawn. "It will be fun to sleep in our little house for the first time! Come on, girls — leave the washing-up till the morning. We are all tired out!"

VII

A STRANGE DISCOVERY

The next day the children went to make sure that their sail-signal was still safely tied to the signal-tree at the top of the cliff. It was. It flapped there steadily, a signal to any passing ship that there were people on the island who needed help.

"Suppose no help comes?" said Tom. "Shall we have to stay here all winter?"

"Yes—unless you like to try and swim dozens of miles back home!" said Andy.

The children looked at one another. Stay there for the winter! It was all very well having an adventure on an island for three or four days—but to stay there all the winter, in the bitter cold and raging storms, was not a pleasant thought.

"Don't look so gloomy," said Andy. "We may be rescued any day. I can't think that no ship ever passes these islands. After all, there were people living here not so long ago—and they must have had supplies from time to time—so the ships must come by here sometimes. And maybe there are people living on one of the other islands. I think perhaps at a very low tide we could cross to the next island by that line of rocks over there—and explore that. We may find dozens of people, for all we know!"

Every one cheered up. Of course! There seemed to be five or six islands near to their own; people would surely be living on one or other of them, especially on the bigger ones. Their own island was so small that it was a wonder anyone had ever bothered to build a house there, and tried to get a living on the rocky soil.

They went to see if their boat was still held fast between the two rocks. Yes—there it was, all on one side, the tide washing right over its decks.

"Perhaps an extra strong tide might lift it off the rocks," said Andy. "If only it would—and we could mend it! I'd try to sail back home again."

"Well, there's nothing left in the boat that could be taken away now," said Tom. "I really think we've got everything movable—ropes, nets, even the oars!"

It was quite true. The boys had brought back with the oil everything in the locker. Ropes might never come in useful—but still, Andy thought they might as well take them. The children thoroughly explored the little island again, but found nothing interesting at all. They could see that the farm-people had used the level stretch of land on the more southerly side of the island for their fields. In one place, Jill found some runner beans growing over a tangle of brambles, and she called out in excitement:

"Beans! We'll eat them for dinner!"

The others came to look. "I expect these seeded themselves too," said Andy. "Maybe there was a bean-field just here. Well—we're not doing too badly, with potatoes and beans and fish!"

There was nothing to do that afternoon, except bathe and fish. The little shack was finished—there was nothing more to add to it. They could do nothing with their wrecked boat. It was of no use going for a ramble for the island was so small. So Tom suggested a bathe first, and fishing afterwards.

It was warm in the sunshiny sea. They swam through the big waves and splashed about lazily. Then they came

out of the sea and lay in the sun to dry. After that, the boys sat on the rocks to fish and the girls went to hunt for prawns, shrimps, and shellfish.

The tide was very low that evening. The wind had completely dropped, and the sea was almost calm—as nearly calm as it ever could be on that rough, rocky coast. The children stood on a rocky ledge, looking to the north where the other islands lay, blue with a summery mist.

"They really look as if they are just floating on the water," said Jill dreamily. "They do look lovely. I wish we could visit them."

"Well, it would be quite easy if we chose low tide," said Andy, pointing to the line of rocks that were now uncovered, and which seemed to lead in a crooked line to the next island. "I'd like fine to go across those rocks to-morrow morning when the tide is low again. We could take food for the day—and see what was on the next island—and climb back across the rocks at low tide to-morrow night."

"Oh, do let's!" cried the twins, and Tom did a little war-dance on the rocky ledge in excitement. Who knew what they might find on the next island?

That night Jill cooked some potatoes in their skins, and let them go cold to take with them next day.

"We'll cook the sausages that are in the tin, let them go cold, and take those, too," said Jill. "We can catch some fish to-morrow night for our evening meal when we come home."

The next morning they ran to see if the tide had uncovered the rocks again. Yes—there they stretched grey and green, some quite bare, some covered with seaweed. Very deep rock-pools lay between. The sea itself lay pale blue and sparkling, beyond the line of rocks.

"Come on!" said Andy. "We'd better go now, before the tide turns."

They leapt down from the ledge and ran to the sandy shore. They jumped up on to the rocks, and then began to make their way carefully over them. Some were so slippery that once or twice the children nearly fell into the deep pools. These pools looked exciting. Quite big fish swam in them, and Andy said big edible crabs would be sure to be there.

"But we've no time for fishing about here," he said. "We shall be caught by the tide if we don't make haste."

Sure enough, the tide was on the turn—but before it could reach the jagged line of rocks over which the children were climbing, they had come to the end of them, and had waded through a pool to the sandy shore of the next island.

"Now we're on island number two!" said Tom, capering about. "Golly! I *am* hungry!"

So was every one. "Well, if we eat all our food now, we shall have to wait ages for our next meal, unless we can find something on this island," said Andy. But he was hungry, too—so they ate their cold sausages and potatoes, and sucked a toffee each.

Then they set off to explore the second island. They turned to climb the cliffs—and had a big surprise!

"Look! Caves!" said Tom, pointing to big black openings in the cliff. "Look at that! Caves of all kinds and sizes and shapes! Let's have a look at them."

They made their way to the first cave—and just outside it Andy stopped and stared at something in the sand.

"What's up?" asked Tom.

"That!" said Andy, and he pointed to a cigarette-end that lay rolling a little in the breeze.

"A cigarette-end!" said Tom, looking all round, as if he were looking for the one who had smoked it. "Well! Somebody has been here all right—and not very long ago, either. But there's not a single house on *this* island, ruined or whole!"

"Perhaps the people live in these caves," said Jill, looking half-timidly at the first one.

"We'll go in and see," said Andy. He pulled a roll of oilskin from his pocket and out of it took a half-candle and a box of matches. Andy never ran any risk of his matches getting wet—and now the children were glad that he was so careful, for no one really wanted to go into the caves without a light of some sort.

Andy lighted the candle and then, leading the way, he stepped into the first cave. The others followed him. The floor was thick with silvery sand, and the walls of the cave were high and smooth. It ran back a long way, and then narrowed into an archway. Through this the children went into another cave, the tiny light of the candle shining on rocky grey walls, and high, rough roof. The floor of the cave then began to go upwards, and became rocky instead of sandy. The cave narrowed into a passage, whose roof was at times so low that they bumped their heads against it.

And then they came to the Round Cave, which was the name they at once gave the last strange cave. It was almost perfectly round, and as the floor slanted down towards the middle, it felt like being inside a hollow ball!

But it wasn't the roundness of the cave that startled the four children — it was what it held!

Piled high everywhere were boxes, sacks, and big tin chests with strange words on them! Some piles reached to the roof of the cave, others reached half-way.

"Golly! Look at that!" said Tom, in the greatest astonishment. "Whatever's in all those boxes and things — and why are they here?"

The little flame of the candle flickered on the strange array in the cave. Andy set the candle gently down on a flat piece of rock, and pulled the neck of a thick brown sack undone. It was lined with coarse blue paper inside. He undid that — and then gave a low cry of surprise.

"Sugar! Stranger and stranger! I was expecting treasure or something — and it's sugar! I wonder what's in the other sacks and boxes."

Some the children could not force open, but others were already opened, as if some one had taken from them some of the contents. The boxes were full of tins—there were tins of soup, meat, vegetables, fruit, sardines—everything one could think of. There was a chest of flour, a chest of tea, tins of salt, even tins of butter and lard, well-sealed and air-tight.

"Andy—I really don't understand this," said Jill in a puzzled voice. "How did all these come here? And who do you suppose they belong to? As far as we know there isn't a single person on the island."

"I don't know any more than you do, Jill," said Andy. "It's like a dream; but anyway we shan't need to starve whilst there's all this food stored here!"

"But may we take it, if it belongs to anyone else?" said Mary, frightened.

"We can pay the person it belongs to," said Andy. "My father and your mother will gladly pay, to keep us from starving, if we have to spend the winter here!"

"Well, come on then—let's take all we want," said Tom, feeling so hungry that he couldn't wait a minute longer. "We'll keep a careful account of everything we take, and pay the bill and a little more, when we find out who owns this very curious larder."

"You're right, Tom," said Andy, in a puzzled voice. "It is a *very*—curious—larder!"

VIII

ODDER AND ODDER

The children each chose what they thought they would like to take away. Sugar they wanted, and salt. The tinned butter would be splendid, and any tins of meat and fruit. Jill thought she might be able to make some rolls of bread with the flour, or, at any rate, some scones. They took tins of powdered milk too, and each child carried quite a heavy load down the narrow passages that led from the Round Cave to the shore-cave.

When they reached the open air Tom took a deep breath and set down his load. "My goodness, it was stuffy up there," he said.

"What puzzles me is why it wasn't *more* stuffy than it was," said Andy. "Air must get into that Round Cave through some hole we didn't see. Pick up your things, Tom, the tide is coming in. We can't stay on this beach. The sea will reach the cave before long."

"It's all right for about ten minutes," said Tom, pulling a fat little notebook from his pocket. "I just want to jot down a list of all the things we've taken, in case we eat them up and then forget what we had."

"Tom's always so honest," said Jill. "Well, I'll tell you the things, Tom, and you can write them down. Three tins of pineapple. One big bag of sugar. Three tins of tongue. Four tins of —"

"Not so fast, not so fast," said Tom, busy writing. He wrote everything down, shut his notebook with a snap, and pushed it back into his pocket. Then he picked up his load and followed Andy up the steep, rocky path.

Until the tide went out that night the children were prisoners on the second island, for there was no way to get back to their own island except by the line of rocks. This was now completely covered by the tide, and great showers of spray were sent high into the air as the water crashed against the rocks over which they had clambered early that day.

"Anyone got a tin-opener?" asked Tom, his mouth watering at the sight of the labels on the tins.

Andy had. In Andy's pockets there was almost anything that anyone could possibly want, from tin-tacks to toffee.

"You'd better open a tin, I suppose," said Andy, with a grin. "I've watched you sticking your finger into the sugar packet a dozen times already—and there'll be none left to take to our island if you do it much more. Open a tin of tongue and perhaps you won't feel so hungry for sugar!"

They all feasted on the tongue, which was really most delicious. They felt very thirsty afterwards, and as they had not found any spring or stream on the second island they could not think what to do.

"Well, why don't we open a tin of pineapple?" said Tom at last. "The chunks will be lovely and juicy and we can all have a drink of the juice in the tin too."

So a tin of pineapple was opened. Both tins were carefully buried by the children, for even though the island seemed quite lonely and deserted they could not bear to make it ugly by leaving empty tins about. The gulls swooped round them all the time they ate, screaming loudly.

Andy imitated them and they grew even more excited,

at last landing on the ground behind the children and waiting there almost within touch.

"These gulls know that where there are people, there may be food," said Andy. "But how do they know that?— these islands seem quite bare and empty."

"And how, how, how did all that food come to be in the Round Cave?" said Jill. "Could it have been there for years, do you suppose—and have been forgotten?"

"No," said Andy. "It hasn't been there very long. The sugar was still soft—and sugar goes hard if it is stored for long. That cigarette-end we found too—that had been smoked not less than a week or two ago, or the wind would have blown it into bits."

"Andy, don't you think it would be a good thing to stay on *this* island and live here, instead of going back to our own island?" asked Mary. "We should be near to a good food-supply then!"

"No, I don't," said Andy, at once. "You forget we have left a signal on our island—and if any ship sees it and calls for us, we might be on *this* island, unable to be rescued because the tide was high and we couldn't get back."

"But couldn't we tie the signal up somewhere on *this* island?" said Tom.

"No," said Andy. "No ship could get to us here. This island is almost surrounded by a reef of the worst rocks I've ever seen. Look at them, right out there."

The children looked. Andy was right. A jagged line of rocks ran some way out from the coast. Between the rocks and the coast the sea lay trapped in a kind of big lagoon or lake, calm and smooth.

Tom frowned and looked puzzled. "Well, if no ship can get in to rescue us if we stay on this island," he said, "how in the world did one get in to land all that food in the cave?"

Andy stared at Tom and looked as puzzled as Tom did. "Yes—that's odd," he said. "Well—maybe there is a way through at high tide. But we can't risk it. We must live on the first island, and when we want food we must come here and get it—and maybe we shall run into the folk who so strangely made a larder in the Round Cave."

Mary stood up and tried to see what the next island was like. It looked much bigger than the first two. There was no line of rocks stretching to it, but only an unbroken spread of blue water. To get to the third island they would have to swim, or use a boat.

"Do you think we'd better leave a note in the cave to say that we are on the first island and would like to be rescued?" said Tom. "The people may come back at any time—and we could go away in their boat."

Andy shook his head. "I think we won't leave a note —or anything else to show we've been here," he said. "There's something a bit mysterious about all this, and if there's a secret going on, we'd better keep out of it till we know what it is."

"Oh, Andy! Whatever do you mean?" cried Mary.

"I don't know what I mean," said Andy. "It's just a feeling I have, that's all. Maybe I'm wrong—but one of us will come over here every day at low tide and just see if there's somebody about before we let them know we're here."

"Well, Andy—what about all our footmarks round the cave?" said Tom.

"The tide will wash all those right away," said Andy. "Look over the cliff-edge, Tom—you will see the tide has gone right into the cave now. There is absolutely nothing that will show we have been there."

"Except that some of the food is missing," said Mary. "You've forgotten that, Andy."

"No, I haven't," said Andy. "There's so much in that cave that I don't think anyone will miss the little we've taken. I don't expect it's checked at all. Nobody would think that any strangers would ever visit that cave."

The children wandered over the island and looked for bilberries, which were fruiting there in great numbers. It was a way of quenching their thirst, to pick the small, juicy bilberries. The island was quite deserted. It did not look as if anyone had ever lived there at all.

The tide went down and the line of rocks began to show. The children clambered down to the shore to go back to their own island. They had tied to their backs the food they had taken, and Andy told everyone to be very careful.

"We don't want to lose our food in a deep pool!" he said. "So don't rush along too fast, Tom. You are always in such a hurry!"

The rocks were wet and slippery, but the children were very careful indeed. Once an extra large wave came and splashed right over Jill, and she gave a squeal.

"Oh, has it wet the food?"

"Yes—soaked it!" called Tom. "But never mind—it's all in tins, Jill."

They got back to their little hut at last and all of them were delighted to see it. It really seemed like coming home.

They sat down on their beds, tired out. But Tom was not going to bed without his supper. He wanted hot soup, more tongue, and a tin of peaches. So the stove had to be lighted, and Tom was sent to fill the kettle.

All the children enjoyed the meal, although they were so sleepy they could hardly bother to clear up afterwards. The first stars were in the sky as they flung themselves on their beds.

"It's awfully early to go to bed," murmured Jill sleepily. "But I can't keep awake another minute!"

And she fell asleep at once. So did Mary. Tom blew out the stove and lay down too. Andy sat up for a while, looking out towards the second island and wondering about a lot of things.

Then he too lay down and fell asleep—but not for long!

A strange and curious noise awoke him. It came into his dreams, startled him and roused him so that he sat up, puzzled and alarmed.

"Tom! Wake up!" said Andy. "Listen to this noise. What is it?"

Tom awoke and listened. "It's a motor-bicycle," he said, half asleep.

"Don't be a fathead!" said Andy. "A motor-bicycle on this island! You're dreaming. Come on, wake up—I tell you there's a jolly queer noise."

The noise itself hummed away into silence. The gulls screamed but soon became quiet. Andy sat and listened a little longer and then, as no more noise came, lay down on his bed again.

"Odder and odder," said Andy to himself. "We seem to have come to some most mysterious islands—and I'm going to find out what's happening—or my name isn't Andy!"

IX

THE MYSTERIOUS VISITORS

The next day the children talked about the queer noise that Andy had heard.

"I tell you it sounded exactly like a motor-bicycle," Tom said firmly, and nothing would make him admit that it wasn't.

"If I didn't know there couldn't possibly be any landing-ground on these rocky islands I might have thought the noise was made by an aeroplane," said Andy thoughtfully. "But that's silly. Why would an aeroplane come here? And where would it land?"

"It might be a motor-boat, perhaps!" said Jill suddenly. The others stared at her. For some reason, nobody had thought of motor-boats till then.

"Yes—I believe it was!" said Andy. "It had that throbbing sound that a motor makes. Now what's a motor-boat doing here? But, anyway—it means that we can be rescued!"

"Of course!" said Tom. "Well—let's go and find the motor-boat. What a surprise they'll get when they suddenly see us! They'll wonder wherever we've come from."

"Tom, don't be in so great a hurry," said Andy, pulling the impatient boy down into the heather. "I think there's something funny going on here—and before we show ourselves we'd better find out if we shall be welcome!"

"Oh," said Tom, surprised. The girls looked rather alarmed.

"What do you mean—something funny?" said Jill.

"I don't know, as I said yesterday," said Andy. "But what we will do is to see where that motor-boat is. It won't have seen our signal because it came in the night — and we know it's not anywhere this side of the island, or we would have seen it this morning. I vote we go to that rocky ledge where we get the best view of the second island and see if by any chance a boat has been able to get through the reef of rocks and sail into the quiet lagoon inside."

The four children made their way to the high rocky ledge.

Andy made them lie down flat and wriggle like Red Indians as they reached it.

"Better not let ourselves be seen, if anyone *is* down there," he whispered. So, as flat as snakes, they wormed their way to the rocky ledge — and when they got there, they had the biggest surprise of their lives!

In the quiet water that lay outside the second island was a large and powerful seaplane!

Yes — a great seaplane, whose wings spread widely over the blue water. No small motor-boat purred there. It was the seaplane's engine that Andy had heard so mysteriously in the middle of the night.

"Whew! Look at that!" whispered Andy, his face going as red as a beetroot with excitement. "I never *thought* of a seaplane! What a very extraordinary thing!"

"Let's get up and shout and wave," begged Jill. "I'm sure they will love to rescue us."

"Haven't you seen the sign on the wings?" asked Tom, in a curiously angry voice. The girls looked. The sign of the crooked cross was painted on each wing — the sign of the enemy, the foe of half the world.

"Golly!" said Mary, and she drew a deep breath.

"Enemies! Using these islands! Do they belong to them?"

"Of course not," said Andy. "But they are desolate, and out of the usual ships' course—and they've been noted by the enemy, and he's using them as a kind of base for something—seaplanes perhaps."

"Well—what are we going to do?" asked Tom.

"We shall have to think," said Andy. "One thing is certain. We won't show ourselves till we've found out a little more. We don't want to be taken prisoners."

"That's what that food was for, then—the people who come here," said Jill. "I suppose the seaplanes come over here for food and petrol. It's a good idea. How I wish we could get away and tell my father about it—he'd know what to do. I guess he'd clean up this place, whatever it's used for!"

"I say—hadn't we better take down our signal whilst that seaplane is here?" asked Jill. "If it happens to see it, the enemy will know there are people on this island. And what about the fishing-boat? That might be seen too."

"I don't think so," said Andy. "It's well hidden between those rocks. But the signal had certainly better come down. We won't put it up any more. Come on, Tom—we'll take it down now."

"We'll come with you," said the girls. But Andy shook his head.

"No," he said. "From now on, somebody must keep a watch on that seaplane. We must find out all we can. We will be back with you as soon as possible—but you must stay here and watch."

So the two girls were left behind whilst the boys ran across the island to take down their flapping signal.

"I don't know where in the world we should hide if we were discovered and hunted for," said Andy, rolling up the sail. "There isn't a single place here to hide away in—not a cave or anything."

Tom felt rather uncomfortable. He didn't want to be hunted for on that bare island! "I wish we could see how many men there are in that seaplane," he said, "and what they are doing, and everything."

"Where are your field-glasses?" asked Andy suddenly. "They would be just the thing to use. We could see everything as clearly as could be, then!"

"And my camera, too!" said Tom, jumping for joy. "What about my camera? We could take some photographs of the seaplane—then everyone would *have* to believe us when we get back—if ever we *do* get back!"

"*That's* a fine idea!" said Andy, really pleased. "Golly! If we could take some pictures of that seaplane with the crooked cross showing up clearly, there wouldn't be the least doubt of our story when we got home. Tom, let's go and get your glasses and your camera straight away."

They dumped the sail into a bush and ran to the shack. They took Tom's field-glasses and picked up the camera to see if it needed a new film. No—there was a new one inside.

"Better not use up all the film on the seaplane," said Andy. "There might be other interesting and extraordinary things to photograph—you never know!"

"Oh, I've got three or four films," said Tom. "I brought plenty with me, thinking I was going to get some good bird pictures, you know. Come on—let's go back to the girls and see what they have to report.

The girls were very glad indeed to see the boys,

and rushed to meet them. They had such a lot to tell.

"Andy! Tom! As soon as you had gone the men in the seaplane put out a funny little round sort of boat," said Jill in excitement. "And they paddled to shore in it, and went to our cave. What a good thing the sea had washed away all our footprints!"

"It was, indeed," said Andy. "Tom, give me the field-glasses. I want to have a look through them."

Andy stared through the powerful glasses. They were so strong that they seemed to bring the seaplane near enough to touch! The boy saw the great crooked crosses boldly painted on the wings. He saw the little rubber

boat left bobbing in the surf, whilst the men visited the cave — either to take something to it, or to bring something away, Andy did not know which.

"There seems to be someone in the seaplane," said Andy. "And, look — there are some men coming from the cave!"

Andy could see them very clearly through his field-glasses — and the others could see them too, though not so well, of course. To them the men looked like faraway dolls.

"They've gone to get food from the cave," said Andy in excitement. "And I guess there's a store of petrol somewhere else for them to get when they want to. Food — and petrol — just what I thought! Using these islands saves enemy planes from having to go hundreds of miles to their own country's stores. My word — we *have* stumbled on to something queer!"

The men entered their rubber boat and rowed back to the seaplane. Twice more they went to the cave and back. Then they climbed up into the plane and disappeared.

"I'm getting most awfully hungry," said Tom at last. "Can't we go and get something to eat?"

"I'll stay here and keep watch, and you and the girls can go and get your dinner," said Andy. "Don't light a fire, whatever you do — the enemy will see the smoke. Use the stove if you want to cook anything. Bring me something to eat and drink later."

"Right," said Tom, and he and the girls wriggled off the high ledge. They stood upright as soon as they were out of sight of the seaplane and tore to their shack.

They ate a hurried meal, and did not cook anything at all. They made up a dinner-packet for Andy and set off to take it to him. But half-way there they heard a noise. R-r-r-r-r-r-r-r! R-r-r-r-r-r-r-r! R-r-r-r-r-r-r! They stopped at once and listened.

"It's the seaplane going off!" cried Tom — and then the sound came again, more loudly than ever. R-R-R-R-R-R-R.

"Look — it's there!" cried Jill. "Drop flat to the ground or we'll be seen!"

Jill had seen the seaplane just rising into the air over the cliff. The three children dropped flat to the ground and lay there perfectly still. The seaplane roared over their island, rose higher and higher, and at last was nothing but a speck in the sky.

"What a narrow escape!" said Tom, sitting up and wiping his forehead. "Golly! My heart did go bump! I've spilt the water I was carrying for Andy. I'll have to get some more!"

"It *was* a shock to see that enormous plane coming!" said Jill. "Oh dear — if we have many more shocks, my hair will turn grey!"

X

AND NOW FOR THE THIRD ISLAND!

The children were very glad that the seaplane had gone. "It's a jolly good thing our signal was taken down before it flew over the island," said Andy, eating the food that the others had brought to him. "I couldn't warn you. It started up its engine all of a sudden, taxied over the smooth water there, and then rose into the air."

"Andy, do you think there's anything to be seen over on the *other* islands?" asked Tom.

"There may be," said Andy. "I think we ought to try and find out. That third island looks a peculiar shape to me — very long indeed, but very narrow. On the other side of it might be a fine natural harbour for seaplanes. There may be heaps there."

"Well, we've only heard one so far," said Tom. "It doesn't seem as if they're very busy, if there *are* lots over there."

"No — you're right, Tom," said Andy. "Well, what about going to see what we can find? I don't quite know how we'll get to the third island — have to swim, I think. I don't believe the girls could swim so far, though."

"I don't think *I* could," said Jill, remembering the long stretch of sea between the second and third islands. "You boys would have to go without us. Mary and I will stay behind and be as patient as we can."

"Shall we go to-morrow?" asked Tom eagerly. "We could cross to the second island at low tide in the morning and swim across to the third island. We could carry a little food with us, wrapped up in your oilskin."

70

"Yes—we'll do that," said Andy. A great feeling of excitement came over the children—a feeling as if some big unknown secret was going to be theirs. Jill shivered a little—it was almost *too* exciting.

"There's one thing I'm worried about," said Andy. "Just suppose we *are* discovered, by any chance—we *must* find some hiding-place."

"Well, there simply isn't any on this island," said Tom. "So we must hope we *won't* be discovered."

Nothing more happened that day. No seaplane came to the calm harbour in the waters of the second island. No sound but the sea-gulls came through the air. It was a lovely day and the children enjoyed themselves bathing and sunning their brown bodies.

Thanks to the store of food they had discovered on the second island they had plenty to eat. Andy caught some nice little fish, and Jill fried them in the tinned butter. They were delicious. Now that they had tinned milk-powder they could make a milk-mixture and use it with their tea or cocoa, and could also sweeten their drinks with the sugar they had brought.

"We are really very well off now!" said Tom, who as usual was thoroughly enjoying his meal. "We'll take another exciting lot of tins away from the Round Cave next time—I saw some baked beans in tomato sauce. I should like those."

The children took turns at keeping watch on the second island from the rocky ledge. But nothing was to be seen at all. They went to bed early because the boys would have rather a hard and long day the next day.

"We shall have to clamber over that line of rocks first," said Andy. "And then we must cross the island and swim to the third one. We shall have to be back on

71

the second island in time to clamber over the rocks at the next low tide. You girls mustn't worry about us. We shall be back all right."

"I do wish we were going too," said Jill. "Don't you think Mary and I could climb over the rocks to the second island and wait for you there? It would be more fun for us to play about there than on this bare island. There are lots of bilberries there we could pick—they are lovely and sweet now."

"All right," said Andy. "But just keep a watch for any seaplane arriving. Lie down flat under a bush or something if you hear one. You mustn't be seen."

"All right," said Mary. "You can trust us to do that."

So the next morning the four children once again climbed over the line of slippery rocks at low tide. The boys had on only their bathing-suits. Andy had tied his oilskin packet safely to his shoulders, and in it was plenty of food for the day. The girls could get what they wanted from the cave.

All four went across the second island, over the heather and bracken to where they could see the third island. It lay in the sea before them, like a long blue and brown snake. Beyond they could see one or two more islands.

"Do you really think you can swim so far, Tom?" asked Mary doubtfully, as she looked at the wide spread of water between the second island and the third.

"Of course," said Tom, who wasn't going to give up this adventure for anything. All the same, the distance was further than he had ever swum before.

"Well—good-bye for the present," said Andy to the girls. "We'll get down to the shore here, wade out as far as we can, and then swim. Have you got Tom's field-glasses, Jill? Good—you can watch us through them all

72

the way to the third island!"

The boys went down to the shore, waded into the water, and then, when they were out of their depth, began to swim. Andy was by far the stronger swimmer —but he kept close to Tom, just in case the younger boy got into difficulties.

On and on they swam, using the breast-stroke because Andy said it was the least tiring. When Tom began to pant a little, half-way across, Andy spoke to him.

"Let's do a spot of floating, Tom. That will rest us a little. It's a long way."

The two boys lay on their backs in the water. It was a little rough and choppy, but quite warm. They floated like logs of wood, spread out flat on the water. It was a fine rest for Tom.

Then once more they swam on—but it began to seem as if Tom would not reach the shore of the third island. His arms felt so tired. His legs seemed to have no push in them. He gasped and panted, and Andy began to feel alarmed.

"Tread water a bit," he called to Tom. "Do you think you'll be able to swim the rest of the way?"

"I don't know," said poor Tom, dreadfully ashamed of himself. But he could *not* seem to make his arms work properly. He was really tired out.

Andy was not in the least tired. He was as strong as a horse, and he trod water beside Tom, wondering what to do.

"Try again, Tom," he said. "It's no use going back! We are more than half-way across."

Tom looked at the cliff of the third island. It seemed a long, long way away still. He tried again, striking out bravely with his tired arms. But after about six strokes

73

he could not swim any more. He turned on his back and floated again.

Andy was really alarmed. "Tom, you can't do any more," he said. "I'll have to help you. I'll swim on my back and you must lie on your front and put your hands on my shoulders. I can drag you along in the water that way, but it will be rather slow."

"Thanks, Andy," said Tom, very angry with his poor swimming, but quite unable to do anything else. He took hold of Andy's shoulders, and Andy, lying on his back with his head towards the third island, began to strike out valiantly with his brown legs.

It was very slow indeed. And now *Andy* began to get tired! Taking two people wasn't nearly so easy as only one, and he began to gasp. *Now* what were they to do? If they both got into difficulties it would be a very serious matter.

It wasn't long before neither Tom nor Andy had any strength left—and goodness knows what would have happened if Andy, striking out desperately with his legs, had not felt something hard beneath him. It was a rock! He felt about with his feet and at last discovered a rock below the water. They had come to a kind of rocky reef rather like the one they had climbed over from their own island to the second one—but this line of rocks was not uncovered by the tide.

"Tom! Tom! Put your feet down and feel where the rocks are!" gasped Andy. "We can stand there—and maybe feel our way along a bit till we come to the sandy bottom."

Tom soon found foothold on the rocks under the water. He felt better at once. He and Andy held hands and together made their way very cautiously over the sunken

rocks, bruising their poor feet, but getting gradually nearer to the shore. And at last they felt the rocks stop, and there was sand beneath their feet! Good.

"Golly! I didn't enjoy that very much," said Tom. "Sorry I was so feeble, Andy."

"It's all right," said Andy. "You did your best. We're all right now."

But in his own mind Andy didn't think they *were* all right! How in the world was he going to get Tom over that stretch of water back to the second island again? He would never, never do it! Andy was very worried indeed.

But he didn't show it. He grinned at Tom, his blue

eyes shining in his wet brown face. "We're here at last!" he said. "And maybe we shall get a few surprises!"

They lay on the sandy shore in the sun for a while, drying themselves. Tom felt very much better after a meal out of the oilskin packet. He almost felt as if he could swim back home again! It was wonderful what food did to Tom.

"I feel a new man now," he said, leaping to his feet. "Come on, Andy, old chap. Let's go up to the cliff-top and go across to the other side of this island, to see if we can spy anything."

Andy got up too. The two boys climbed up the rough cliff and sat on the top to get back their breath. The island seemed to be about the same as the other two—covered with heather, bracken and grass, and with white gulls soaring over it.

They crossed the narrow width of the island and at last came to the cliff on the other side.

"Wriggle along on the ground now, just in case there's anyone about," said Andy. So both boys wriggled along on their fronts, and came at last to a place where they could see down to the water far below.

And what they saw there filled them with such astonishment and alarm that for at least five minutes neither boy could say a word!

XI

THE SECRET OF THE ISLANDS

The sight that the two boys looked down upon was hardly to be believed. There was a very fine natural harbour of extremely deep water on the north-eastern side of the third island—and lying in this water were at least seven or eight submarines!

Submarines! A submarine base in those deserted islands! No wonder so many of our ships had been sent to the bottom in the waters around these islands!

"It's a real nest of submarines," whispered Andy at last. "Enemy submarines! I can't believe it. My word, Tom, we've stumbled on an amazing secret."

The boys lay looking down on the water. Some of the submarines lay like great grey crocodiles, humped out of the water. One or two were moving out of the harbour, their periscopes showing. It was a curiously silent place, considering that so many of these underwater ships were there. There was no noise of shouting—no noise of machinery—just a dull throbbing every now and again.

"They get fuel and food here," whispered Andy. "They are the small submarines—this harbour can easily take a dozen or more. It's a perfect place for submarines. Do you see how they haven't built any jetties or piers—not a thing that anyone could see, if one of our own planes came over? All they would have to do then would be to sink under the water—and then there would be nothing to see. They store everything in the caves—golly, it's amazing."

For a very long time the two boys lay watching the strange sight below. Two submarines slipped silently out of the harbour entrance — a way between two reefs of high rocks. A third submarine came in, and lay peacefully with the others, the men coming out on the deck and looking around.

At first Tom had been so full of surprise and alarm, so swept with excitement, that he could think of nothing but the sight of the queer vessels. Then another thought came into his head and he turned to Andy.

"Andy," he said. "We've *got* to get home and tell what we've seen."

"I know," said Andy. "I'm thinking that too, Tom. And we've got to get the girls off these islands. We are all in danger. If the enemy knew we were spying on them like this I don't know what would happen to us."

"I don't care how much danger we're in," said Tom, and he didn't. "All I know is that we've *got* to go and tell our people at home about this submarine base. It's got to be cleared away. Andy, it's serious."

Andy nodded. Both boys seemed to become men at that moment. They looked gravely into each other's eyes and what they saw there pleased them both. Each boy knew that the other would do his best and even more than his best.

"Do you think we shall be believed if we go home with a story like this?" said Tom. "Grown-ups have some funny ideas sometimes. They might think we had made it all up — or been mistaken."

"We'll get your camera and take a few photographs," said Andy. "Nobody can disbelieve photographs. And another thing we must do is to try to do something with our boat. We *must* get it off the rocks somehow and try

78

to patch it up. It's our only way of getting back home."

They watched the harbour for a little while longer, and then wriggled along the top of the cliff till they came to some bushes. They went down by these and ran along till they came to the end of the harbour. Beyond lay a cove, and in it, drawn up to the sand, were a number of small boats. No one seemed to be about.

The sight of the little boats excited Andy. If only he could get hold of one! Then he and Tom could row round the third island, and get back to the second one safely. Andy knew perfectly well that Tom could not swim back—and he did not mean to leave the boy alone on this submarine island.

"Tom," he said, "see those boats? Well, what about waiting till night-time—and then stealing down to the cove and taking a boat? We could easily row it back to the second island. It would save us having to swim—and we might even fill it with food and water and try our luck at going home. I could fix up the sail somehow."

"Good idea, Andy," said Tom, his face glowing with excitement. "But I say! Won't the girls be awfully worried if we don't swim back before low tide tonight?"

"We'll go to the cliff on the other side of this island and wave to them," said Andy. "They've got the field-glasses and will see us quite clearly. We'll point and wave and nod and try to show them that our plans are altered, but that we're all right."

"Good," said Tom. "Let's go now. I feel so awfully excited that I really must do something!"

The boys went to the other side of the island. After a while the girls appeared and waved to them. Jill put the glasses to her eyes.

"The boys seem frightfully pleased and excited about

something!" she said. "They are waving and pointing and nodding like anything. They seem to want us to understand something."

"Well, it can only be that they have found something exciting and are going to do something about it," said Mary, taking the glasses from Jill and looking through them. "Yes—Tom's like a mad thing. Well, we shall know when they come back tonight. I only hope Tom will be able to swim back all right. I was really afraid he'd drown this morning."

The boys disappeared after a time. They sat down in a little sunny hollow and finished the rest of the food. Andy found a stream of water and the boys drank from it. Then they sat talking quietly, waiting for the night to come.

At last it came. The moon was behind the clouds, and gave only a pale light now and again. The boys slipped quietly to the top of the cliff that overlooked the small cove next to the harbour. They had already planned the easiest way down. Andy went first. He climbed like a cat. Tom followed him, trying not to send any stones clattering down the cliff.

They came to the shore. It was sandy and their feet made no noise. The boys stayed in the shadow of the cliffs for a few minutes, listening. They could hear no noise at all, except the small sound of little waves breaking on the sand. The boats were not far off, upturned in a row. No one was guarding them. Indeed, why should anyone? No one had ever set foot on the islands since the farm-folk had gone—save for the crews of enemy seaplanes and submarines.

The boys crept over the silvery sand. "Take the boat on the left," whispered Andy. "It's just our size."

They came to the boat—and then they heard voices. They seemed to come from the far side of the cliff, and sounded clearly in the night. The boys could not hear any words—but the sound was enough to make them lie down flat beside the boat they had chosen.

Tom was trembling. Suppose they were found out just as they were taking the boat! It would be too bad. The boys listened until the sound of voices died away and then they cautiously lifted their heads.

"When the moon gets into that very thick cloud we'll turn the boat over and run her into the water," whispered Andy. "You take this side and I'll take the other. Be ready."

"Right," whispered back Tom. So when the moon slipped behind the dark clouds the boys rose silently to their feet. They turned over the boat with hardly a sound, though it was awkward and heavy. Then they pulled it over the sand to the water. Tom got in and took the oars. Andy pushed the boat right out and leapt in himself. The moon was still hidden.

Silently the boys rowed away from the shore, hoping that the moon would remain behind the cloud until they had pulled out of sight. No shout was heard. No running feet. They were undiscovered, so far!

They rowed fast. When the moon came out again they were far from the little cove. "Look! Pull round a bit more," said Andy. "We're passing round the end of the island. We've done well to get here so quickly!"

Soon they were right round the narrow end of the third island. They rowed into the broad stretch of water between the second and third islands. Then across to the shore below the cliff where they had left the girls.

Jill and Mary were watching there. They had been

81

very worried when night had come and brought with it no boys. They couldn't imagine what had happened. They were in a great state of alarm and fright.

And then Jill, looking through the glasses when the moon had swum out into a clear piece of sky, had seen a little boat coming into the stretch of water between the two islands. She clutched Mary's arm.

"Look! A boat! Is it the enemy?"

The girls looked and looked, their hearts beating loudly. They could not see who was in the boat. It landed on the beach—and then the call of a seagull floated up the cliff.

"Andy!" cried Jill, nearly falling down the cliff. "It's Andy! I'd know his seagull call anywhere!"

The boys climbed up the cliff and came to the rocky ledge. The girls fell on them and hugged them like bears, they were so relieved to see them.

"The boat! Where did you get the boat?" cried Jill.

"What did you see? What did you find?" cried Mary.

"We'll tell you all about it," said Andy, and the four of them sat close together on the cold, windy ledge, quite forgetful of the chilly breeze, talking and listening eagerly.

The girls could hardly believe the boys' story. It seemed quite impossible.

"And now that we've got a boat, we'll fill it full of food and water, and see if we can get home," said Andy. "It's the only thing we can do—and we must do it."

"But, Andy," said Jill, "just suppose the enemy see their boat is missing—won't they take alarm and search the islands?"

"Yes—they certainly will," said Andy. "And so we must start to-morrow. We will have a good sleep tonight—

take plenty of food from the cave — and see if we can make for home."

"If only we can get away before the enemy finds that boat is missing!" said Tom. "Oh, do you suppose we shall?"

XII

A DARING ADVENTURE

The children did not have a very good night after all, for they were far too excited to sleep. They had all rowed in the stolen boat to their own island, and had landed there, tied up the boat and gone to their shack.

They slept rather late the next morning, for not one of them had gone to sleep before midnight — and they were awakened by the throbbing noise that they had heard two nights before!

"The seaplane again!" said Andy, waking up at once and leaping to his feet. He ran to the open doorway of the hut, and was just in time to see the plane soar overhead. Then it went round in great circles ready to land on the smooth water outside the second island.

"That means we can't get away today," said Tom at once. "We simply *must* get food into the boat — and we can't if that plane is there."

"No — we can't," said Andy. "But I tell you what we might do, Tom. We might row to the third island, tie our boat up in a hidden place, creep to the top of that cliff, and try to take a few photographs of the submarine bay! We meant to take some photos, you know."

"Yes—we could do that," said Tom. "We'll have to be pretty careful, though."

"We will be," said Andy. "Jill, what is there for breakfast?"

There were tinned sausages and baked beans and tomato sauce. Jill proudly produced some little rolls of bread she had made too. They all ate in silence, thinking over everything that had happened.

"That seaplane may not stay long," said Andy. "It didn't last time. I expect it has come to add to the stores —or maybe take away from them. It will be busy that side of the island—so we will row round the *other* side, where we won't be seen, go across to the third one, and tie up there. You girls must stay here."

"Oh, you always have the exciting things to do," sighed Mary. "Can't we really come with you? I don't see why we can't."

"Well, if you promise to do exactly what you're told, you can come," said Andy, after a minute's thought. He didn't really like the idea of leaving the girls all alone again. Perhaps it would be better if they came.

The girls were thrilled. They cleared away the breakfast things and washed up. They prepared a meal to take with them. It was a very good thing they had discovered that store cave—they now had plenty of food of all kinds. They did hope the seaplane wouldn't take everything away!

They all got into the boat. The boys rowed off, and were careful to keep to the side opposite the cave when they came to the second island. They rowed quickly over the space of water separating that island from the third one, and came to the farthest tip of it. Here there was a tiny beach with steep, overhanging cliffs—so overhanging that it almost seemed as if a big piece was about to fall off!

"Just the place," said Andy, pulling into the tiny beach. "Jump out, girls. Take the food with you. Give a hand with the boat, Tom. We'll run it up the beach and put it right under that dangerous piece of cliff. It will be well hidden there."

They put the boat there and looked at it. The end of it jutted out and could be seen. Jill ran to a seaweed-covered rock and pulled off handfuls of the weed.

"Let's make the boat into a rock!" she said, with a laugh. "Cover it with seaweed!"

"Jolly good idea!" said Andy. "I didn't know girls could have such good ideas!"

"You wait and see what fine ideas we have!" said Mary. They all pulled at the seaweed, and soon the boat was nicely draped and looked so exactly like a seaweed-covered rock that no one could possibly guess it wasn't, even if they passed quite near it.

"That's good," said Andy. "Now we'll make our way very carefully across this end of the island till we come to the little cove where we took our boat from. We'll just peep over the cliff and see if there's anyone there looking as though they have missed the boat! Then we'll crawl to the top of the next cliff that overlooks the submarine bay, and Tom shall take a few pictures."

Everything went well. Keeping close to tall bushes of gorse and bramble, the four children crept over the tip of the island and soon came to the cliff below which was the boat-cove. Cautiously Andy parted some bramble sprays and peeped down to the beach below.

There were the rest of the little boats, still upturned. Nobody was about at all. As far as Andy could see, the stolen boat had not been missed. Good!

Andy let the rest of the children look down to the beach. Tom was pleased. "As long as our boat isn't missed we are all right," he said. "I should think the enemy feel they are so safe here that it just doesn't enter their heads that a boat might be taken. I don't believe they'll ever miss it."

"I hope you're right," said Andy. "But it doesn't do to think the enemy is careless or stupid. We must think they are smart and clever, and try to be the same ourselves. Now let's wriggle along to the next bit of cliff—and you girls can see the submarines. That will be a sight for you!"

Going very slowly and cautiously indeed the four of them made their way under bushes and bracken to the top of the next cliff. They all lay on their tummies and peeped between the tall bracken. The girls drew a long breath of surprise.

"Golly!" said Jill. "One—two—three—four—five—six —seven—however many submarines are there? And all of them marked with the crooked cross."

"An enemy submarine base so near our own land!" said Mary. "And nobody knows it!"

"Where's your camera, Tom?" whispered Andy. Tom had it round his shoulder. Carefully he took it out of its waterproof case and set it for taking distant pictures.

"It's got the seaplane on the first two negatives," said the boy in a low tone. "I'll fill up the rest of the film with photos of the submarines. The pictures can easily be made larger when we get home. Then nobody can disbelieve us, or say we made it all up!"

Click! went the camera. "One picture taken," said Tom. "I got in those two big submarines together, just over there."

Click! Click! Click! Click! Tom was as careful as he could be to take good photographs. Soon the whole film was used. "I'll wait till I get back to the hut and then I'll wind off the film in a dark corner," said the boy. "That's a spot of good work done!"

He put the camera back into its case and strapped it up. The four children lay and looked at the nest of submarines in the water below. Another came slipping in as they watched. Two slipped out.

"Gone to sink some more of our ships, I suppose," said Andy angrily. "If only I could stop them! But we will clean up the whole lot once we get the news back

home. I guess we'll have a battleship or two sent out here."

"Where will it be safe to have something to eat?" asked Tom. "I do feel hungry."

"I wish I had five pence for every time I've heard Tom say that," said Jill, with a giggle.

"Well, I only say what the rest of you are thinking!" said Tom. "I bet you're all hungry!"

They were! Andy found a little bracken dell not far from the top of the cliff. Here the bracken was taller than the children, and once they had settled themselves down below the tall fronds nobody could possibly see them either from above or passing by.

They ate a good meal and enjoyed it. They lay on their backs and looked between the fronds at the blue sky. It was marvellous that the weather was still so good. It would have been miserable if it had rained all the time.

"Now we'd better get back," said Andy.

"Oh, why?" asked Jill, lazily. "I was almost asleep."

"I'll tell you why!" said Andy. "Supposing that stolen boat is missed — well, the first place searched would be this island! And we'd be found. No — the best thing for us to do is to get back now, wait till the seaplane has left and then go straight to the store-cave and fill our boat with food. Then we'll start off tonight."

"All right. We'll come along now then," said Jill, getting up. They took one last peep at the submarine bay and another at the boat-cove. Then they made their way very cautiously back to the tiny beach where they had hidden their boat.

It was still there, beautifully draped with seaweed. Nobody had discovered it! The children dragged it down to the waves and jumped into it. Andy pushed it out.

They took turns at rowing. They were half-way round the second island, on the coast opposite to the one where the store-cave was, when a dreadful thing happened.

The seaplane chose that minute to leave the water by the second island and to rise into the air, ready to fly off!

The children had no time to rush their boat into shore and hide. They were out on the sea, clearly to be seen!

"Crouch down flat in the boat, so that the pilot may perhaps think there's nobody in it," ordered Andy. They shipped the oars quickly and crouched down. The seaplane rose up high, and the children hardly dared to breathe. They did so hope it would fly off without noticing them.

But it suddenly altered its course and began to circle round, coming down lower. It flew down low enough to examine the boat, and then, rising high, flew over the third island, and then flew down to the submarine bay.

Andy sat up, his face rather pale under its brown.

"That's done it," he said. "They saw us! Now they'll count their boats—find there's one missing—and come to look for us!"

XIII

TOM DISAPPEARS

The children looked at one another in the greatest dismay. To think the seaplane should have flown over just at that very moment! It was too bad.

"Well, we can't sit here looking at one another," said Andy, in a brave voice. "We've got to do something quickly. But what? I can't seem to think!"

Nobody could think what to do. Andy longed desperately for some grown-up who could take command and tell him what would be the best thing to do. But there was no grown-up. This was something he had to decide himself—and he must decide well, because the two girls were in his care.

"We had better row straight round to the store-cave and fill the boat with food whilst we can," he said at last. "Then we'll start out straightaway and hope that the seaplane won't spot us out on the sea. It's the only thing to do."

It was a long row round to the cave, but they got there at last, quite tired out. There was nobody about. They beached the boat and jumped out. It was not long before they were in the Round Cave, carrying out stacks of tins and boxes to the boat.

"Golly! We've got enough food to last for weeks!" said Tom.

"We may need it!" said Andy. "Goodness knows how far it is back home. I've not much idea of the right direction either, but I shall do my best."

Tom staggered out to the boat with heaps of things. Andy looked at the pile of food at the end of the boat and nodded his head.

"That's enough," he said. "We don't want to make the boat too heavy to row! Get in!"

They all got in. They rowed out beyond the reef of rocks where they had found a way in and then towards their own island. Andy wanted to get the rugs, for he was sure they would be bitterly cold at night.

"You girls jump out and go and fetch all the warm things you can find," said Andy. "And bring a cup or two and a knife. I've got a tin-opener."

The girls sped off to the shack in the hollow—and whilst they were gone the boys heard the sound they dreaded to hear—the noise of seaplane engines booming over the water!

"There it comes again!" said Andy angrily. "Always at the wrong moment. Lie down flat, Tom. I hope the girls will have the sense to do the same!"

The seaplane zoomed down low over the island, as if it were hunting for someone. Then it droned over the sea, and flew round in great circles. Andy lifted his head and watched it.

"You know what it's doing?" he said. "It's flying round hunting the sea for our boat—just as a hawk flies over fields hunting for mice! It's a good thing we didn't set out straightaway. I think now we'd better wait for the night to come—and then set out in the darkness. We should be seen as easily as anything if we try to go now."

They waited till the drone of the plane's engines was far away. It was hunting the waters everywhere for the stolen boat. Andy stood up and yelled to the girls, who were lying flat under a bush.

"It's gone for the moment. Help us to take out these goods and hide them. If the boat is discovered here and taken away, and we are made prisoners on this island, we shall at least be sure of stores!"

"If we are able to start out tonight we can easily put back the food," said Tom. They all worked hard, and buried the tins and boxes under some loose sand at the top of the beach. They pulled the boat farther up the beach and then sat down to rest, hot and tired.

And then poor Tom gave a squeal of dismay. The others jumped and looked at him in fright. "Whatever's the matter?" asked Andy.

"My camera!" said Tom, his face a picture of horror. "My camera—with all those pictures I took! I left it in the store-cave."

"Left it in the *store*-cave!" said everyone. "Whatever for?"

"Well, I was afraid I'd bump it against the rocks, carrying it up and down those passages," said Tom. "So I took it off for a minute, meaning to put it on when we went. And I forgot."

"You fathead!" said Jill.

"Don't call me that," said poor Tom, looking almost ready to cry.

"Well, fathead is too good a name," said Mary. "Thinhead would be better. You can't possibly have got any brains if you do a thing like that, so you must be a thinhead with no brains at all."

Tom went very red. He blinked his eyes and swallowed a lump that had suddenly come into his throat. He knew how valuable the pictures were that he had taken. How *could* he have come to forget his camera like that?

"Cheer up, Tom," said Andy. "I know what you feel

like. I felt just like that when I found I'd forgotten to bring the anchor in the ship. It's awful."

Tom was grateful to Andy for not scolding him. But all the same he felt really dreadful. They had gone to such a lot of trouble to get those photographs — and now all because of his carelessness they had been left behind.

"I vote we have something to eat," said Andy, thinking that would cheer Tom up. But it didn't. For once in a way Tom had no appetite at all. He couldn't eat a thing. He sat nearby looking gloomily at the others.

The seaplane did not come back. The children sat and waited for the evening to come, when they might start. Jill yawned. "I must do something for the next two or three hours," she said, "or I shall fall asleep. I think I'll take the kettle and keep filling it with water at the spring, and bring it back to the boat. There's a big water-barrel there, and we could fill it with water."

"Good idea," said Andy. "You and Mary do that. I think I'll just wander up to the bush where we put the sail and see if it's still there. I don't think I've time to rig up some kind of a mast in this little boat so the sail won't be any good. But it might be useful to cover us with if it should happen to pour with rain."

The girls went off. Andy nodded to Tom, who was still looking gloomy, and went across the island to the bush where he had put the sail.

Tom was left alone. "They don't want me with them," thought the boy, quite wrongly. "They think I'm awful. *I* think I'm awful too! Oh, dear — if only I could get my camera."

He thought of the reef of rocks that led to the second island. It wasn't a bit of use trying to climb over them because the tide was getting high now.

But then he thought of the boat! It really wasn't a great distance to row to the cave, from the beach where he was. How pleased the others would be, if he got back his camera!

The boy did not stop to think. He dragged the boat down the beach by himself, though he nearly pulled his arms out, doing it! He pushed it into the water and jumped in. He took the oars and began to row quickly round to the second island. He would land on the shore then, run quickly to the cave and get his camera.

"Then I'll be back here with it almost before the others know I'm gone!" he thought.

Nobody would have known what Tom had done if Andy had not happened to look round as he went over the little island to find the old sail. To his enormous astonishment he saw their boat being rowed away!

He could not see that the one in it was Tom, and for a moment he stood still, wondering what had happened. Was it another boat, not their own? He ran quickly to find out.

He soon saw that it was their own boat. He saw where Tom had dragged it down the beach. He could just see the boat rounding the corner of a cliff now.

"That was Tom all right," said Andy to himself. The girls came back at that moment and shouted to Andy.

"What's the matter? Why do you look like that? Where's the boat?"

"Tom's gone off with it," said Andy angrily.

"*Tom!* Whatever do you mean, Andy?" asked Jill in the greatest surprise.

"I suppose he felt upset about leaving his camera behind and he's gone to get it by himself," said Andy.

"He really is a fathead. He may be seen and caught. I'm quite sure someone will be hunting for us soon. Really, I could shake Tom till his teeth rattled!"

The girls stared at Andy in dismay. They did not at all like the idea of their brother going off alone in the boat. Well—they would just have to wait patiently till Tom came back. It should not really take him a very long time. The sun was sinking now. He should be back by the time it was gone. Then they could all start out again and try to make for home.

Jill set the kettle of water down on the beach. She felt tired. Mary sat down beside her and looked out over the water for Tom to come back. Andy walked up and down impatiently. He could understand that Tom longed to get back his camera and put himself right with the others so that they no longer thought him careless and silly—but he did wish he hadn't gone off in their precious boat!

The three children waited and waited. The sun sank lower. It disappeared over the sky-line and the first stars glimmered in the darkening sky.

And still Tom was not back. The girls could no longer see anything on the sea, which was now dark. They could only sit and listen for the plash of oars.

"Tom ought to be back by now," said Andy anxiously. "He's had plenty of time to get a dozen cameras! Whatever is he doing?"

Nobody knew. They sat there on the chilly beach, anxious and worried. If only, only Tom would come back! Nobody would scold him. Nobody would grumble at him. They just wanted him to come.

"I should think he's been caught," said Andy at last. "There can't be any other reason why he's not back. *Now* we're in a pretty fix! No Tom—and no boat!"

XIV

A PRISONER IN THE CAVE

What had happened to Tom? A great many things. He had rowed safely to the beach where the caves lay hidden in the cliff behind. He had dragged the boat up the sand and had gone into the first cave. He stumbled through the rocky archway and into the queer Round Cave, which was so full of food.

He had no torch, so he had to feel around in the dark for his camera. It took him a long time to find it.

"Where *did* I put it?" wondered the boy anxiously. "Oh, if only I had a match!"

But he hadn't. He felt over tins and boxes — and at last his hand fell on the box-like shape of his camera, safe in its waterproof covering!

"Good," Tom thought. "Now I'll just rush down to the boat and row back. I really must be quick or the others will be worried."

But Tom had a dreadful shock as he was about to make his way out of the Round Cave back to the beach. He heard voices!

The boy stood perfectly still, his heart beating fast. Whose voices were these?

They came nearer. Men were on the beach outside! Men had found his boat! Was it the enemy?

Alas for poor Tom — it *was* the enemy! Tom had not heard the boom of the seaplane coming down on the water. He had not seen a rubber boat putting off hurriedly to the cave. But now he could hear the voices of the men.

They had seen the boat on the beach, and had come to examine it. They soon saw that it was the stolen boat, which had now been missed and was being searched for.

The men knew at once where the owner of the boat was—in the cave! And they were going to search for him there.

Tom darted back into the Round Cave and hid behind a big pile of boxes. He felt quite certain he would be found—and as he crouched there, trembling and excited, he made up his mind very, *very* firmly that he would not say how many others had come to the islands with him. He would make the men think that he was the only one —then maybe the other three would not be hunted for.

"I've been a perfect silly to run into danger like this," thought poor Tom. "But, at any rate, I can save the others from being hunted for, perhaps."

The men came into the Round Cave. They had powerful torches which they flashed around—and almost at once they saw Tom's feet sticking out from behind a box.

They dragged him out and stood him up. They seemed most astonished to find only a boy. They had expected a man. They talked quickly among themselves in a language that Tom could not understand.

Then one man, who could talk English, spoke to Tom. "How did you get to this island?"

"I set off in a sailing-boat and a storm blew up and wrecked me," said Tom. "You can see my boat off the coast of the next island, if you look."

"Is there anyone else with you on this island?" asked the man. "Speak the truth."

Tom could reply quite truthfully that there *was* no one else with him on the island!

Thank goodness, the others were on the first island!

"There isn't anyone else here with me," he answered. "Search the cave, and see!"

The men did search the cave again, but found nobody, of course. They did not seem satisfied, however. Tom could see that they felt sure there were others to find.

"How did you find this cave?" asked the man who spoke English.

"By accident," said Tom.

"And I suppose you also found our boat by accident, and saw the submarines by accident?" said the man, in a very nasty voice. "Are you sure there is no one else here with you?"

"Quite sure," said Tom. "Wouldn't you see them in the cave, if there were?"

"We shall not take your word for it," said the man, with a horrid laugh. "We shall search this island and both those next to it—and if we find anyone else, you will be very, very sorry for yourself!"

"You won't find anyone!" said Tom, hoping to goodness that they wouldn't, and wishing he could warn Andy and the girls somehow. "Are you going to keep me prisoner?"

"We certainly are," said the man. "And as you seem so fond of this cave, we'll let you stay here! You've food to eat—and you won't be able to do any spying round if you're here in this cave! We shall put a man on guard at the entrance—so if you try to get out, or anyone else tries to get in, you'll be caught. Our man will be well hidden behind a rock at the entrance—and if any friends of yours try to rescue you, they will get a shock!"

Tom listened, his heart sinking into his shoes. What an idiot he had been! He was to be a prisoner—and if the others tried to find him they would be made prisoners too, for they would never guess a sentry was hidden behind the rocks, watching for them.

Tom sat down on a box. He would not cry. He would not show the men how frightened and worried he was. His face was brave and bold—but inside he felt as if he was crying buckets of tears! If only, only he could get word to Andy!

There was nothing he could do—nothing! He could only sit there in the cave, surrounded by marvellous food that he felt too worried even to look at, and think about the others. Poor Tom! It was a dreadful punishment for being careless enough to forget his camera, and foolish enough to try and fetch it!

The men left a lamp in the cave for Tom. It was getting late and the boy was tired—but he could not sleep. He heard the men go out, and he knew a sentry had been placed by the rocks. He could not hope to escape. But he could try!

So, very quietly, he made his way through the rocky archway, down to the shore-cave below. But his feet set the stones moving here and there, and a voice came out of the darkness.

He could not understand what was said to him, but the voice was so stern that the boy fled back to the Round Cave at once. It wasn't a bit of good trying to escape.

He sat down again and wondered about the others. What were they thinking and doing? Would they guess he had gone to fetch his camera, and come to look for him when the tide uncovered the rocks next day? If so, they would certainly be caught.

Andy and the girls sat up until they could keep awake no longer. They went back to the shack, curled up on their beds, and slept restlessly, worrying about Tom and the lost boat.

In the morning, Andy went out cautiously, wondering if the enemy had already landed a boat on their island to hunt for them. But he could see nothing strange.

He sat talking to the girls as they prepared breakfast. "Tom is certainly caught," he said. "There's no doubt about that, I'm afraid. Well, I know enough of Tom to know that he won't say *we* are here, too. He won't give us away. But they will certainly come and hunt for anyone else who might be here. We have to do two things—hide ourselves so that we can't *possibly* be found—and then think of some way of rescuing Tom."

"Oh dear! It seems quite impossible," said Jill, feeling very worried. Mary began to cry.

"Don't cry, Mary," said Andy, putting his arm round her. "We have to be brave now. We are British children, and so we have plenty of courage and heaps of ideas. We must all think hard and see what we can do to trick the enemy."

"But, Andy, how can we hide on this bare island?" said Mary, drying her eyes and blinking away her tears. "They will beat all through the bracken and heather. There are no good trees to hide in. Not a single cave. Really, there isn't anywhere at all!"

"You're right, Mary," said Andy. "It's going to be very difficult. But we must think of *some*thing. You see, if only we can hide and not be found we can *some*how think of a way to rescue Tom—but if we are found we can't help Tom, and won't be able to escape and tell our secret!"

"Yes—it's very, very important," said Jill thoughtfully. "Let's think of ways of hiding. The bracken is no use at all, is it?"

"Not a bit of use," said Andy. "I did think we might perhaps wade out to the ship and hide down in the cabin —but I know they would look there."

"Could we hide in the shack?" asked Mary. "Pile the the heather over ourselves, or something?"

"No," said Andy. "We should be discovered there at once. And there's no place in any of the other buildings. I wish we knew of a cave or something like that."

"It's a good thing we've got plenty of food hidden in the sand," said Jill. "If we *can* manage to hide ourselves away we need not starve! We've only got to go and dig up that store of food!"

"Yes — that's very lucky," said Andy. "I say, listen! That's the sound of a motor-boat, isn't it?"

Andy crept out to see, keeping well under cover. Yes — there was a motor-boat coming round the corner of the island — a motor-boat with five men in it!

"They're coming!" whispered Andy. "They're in a motor-boat. Quick — where shall we hide!"

"We'd better rush over to the opposite side of the island," said Jill, her face pale. "The first place they'll hunt is this side, where they land. Quick, Mary!"

The three children slipped out of the shack and made their way up the rocky path. They were just out of sight when the motor-boat landed on the beach. They would be able to reach the other side of the island unseen but what could they do there? The shore there was nothing but rocks and sand — they would be found in two minutes!

XV

THE ISLAND IS SEARCHED

Andy and the girls did not take long to reach the opposite shore of the island. They slid down the steep cliff there and reached the beach. It was sandy, but at one side was a mass of seaweed-covered rocks. It was impossible to hide behind them, for a moment's search would at once discover them.

They looked at one another in despair. "Any good wading out to sea and keeping under water?" asked Jill.

"No," said Andy, "we'd have to keep popping our heads up to breathe and we'd be seen at once."

Jill stared at the rocks nearby and then she gave such a squeal that Andy and Mary jumped in fright.

"Sh!" said Andy angrily. "You'll be heard. Whatever's the matter?"

"I've thought of how to hide!" said Jill breathlessly. "It's the same idea I had for hiding that boat. Can't we cover ourselves with sand, and then drape ourselves with seaweed, to look like rocks? We could go and lie down beside those rocks, and if we were well covered with weeds we'd look exactly like them!"

"Golly! That *is* an idea!" said Andy at once. "Quick! I'll cover you girls with sand at once. Come over here."

The three ran to the rocks. The tide was out, and the sand was hard but damp. Andy made the girls lie down together, and then he piled sand high over them, leaving a space over their noses for breathing. He only had his hands to do this, so it was hard work. Then he dragged great handfuls of seaweed from the rocks and threw it over the sandy mound. When he had finished, the girls looked exactly like the seaweed-covered rocks nearby! It was really marvellous.

Andy covered with loose seaweed the untidy places he had made in the sand. Then he began to make a hole for himself, and to cover himself too. He draped himself with piles of seaweed and then poked up his head to look at the girls.

He really didn't know which of the rocks they were! He simply couldn't tell! He looked and looked — but not until one of the rocks moved a little did he see that it was the girls!

"Jill! Mary!" he called in a low voice. "As soon as you hear me screaming like a gull you must lie absolutely still. You look marvellous! I didn't know which rock you were till one of you moved."

"Andy, I'm afraid one of the men might tread on me," said Mary, in a frightened voice.

"Well, let him!" said Andy. "I don't advise you to call out and ask him not to walk on you!"

There was a little giggle from the nearby rock. Although the girls were frightened they could still see a joke. They all lay quietly for a time and then Andy heard voices coming near. He cried like a seagull, and the girls then lay so still that not even the tiniest bit of seaweed above them moved at all.

The men slid down to the sandy shore, calling to one another in loud voices. Andy could not understand anything they said. All the children's hearts beat loudly and Jill wondered if hers could possibly be heard. It seemed to her to be thumping as loudly as a hammer.

The men stood on the beach and looked round. One

shouted something to the others and began to walk over to the rocks. Andy felt most alarmed.

"I do hope we look like real rocks," he thought. "And I hope nobody treads on us—we should be found at once if that happened—to say nothing of being hurt!"

The man came nearer. He stood near Andy and took out a packet of cigarettes. Andy heard him strike a match and knew that he had lighted a cigarette.

The man threw the empty cigarette packet on to the sand, and puffed at his cigarette. A young gull, seeing the man throw the packet away, thought that it might be a piece of bread. It flew down to see, crying "Ee-oo, ee-oo, ee-oo!" very loudly.

The other gulls heard it and soared round in circles, wondering if there was any food to find. The young gull landed on the sand and stood looking at the packet, hardly daring to go nearer to peck it, for it was too close to the man.

The other gulls flew down—and two stood on Andy and one stood on the girls! The children looked so exactly like rocks that the gulls really thought they were!

One gull thought the rock felt unusually soft and warm and he bent down his head and pecked at it. He pecked Andy's knee and the boy nearly gave a yell.

The men joined the one who was smoking a cigarette. They did not even bother to walk over the rocks. One man said that it was plain there could be nobody hiding there for the gulls would not stand about as they were doing if there was anyone hiding. They would know it and be suspicious.

For some time the men stood talking and smoking. Then they turned to go up the cliff again. One walked so near Andy that the boy could feel the thud of his footfall close by. Up the cliff climbed the men and disappeared over the top.

Andy cautiously lifted his head after a while and looked around. There was no one to be seen.

The boy felt that it would be safer if they all stayed where they were for some time longer—but he felt cold and damp, and he was afraid that the girls would catch a dreadful chill.

"Mary! Jill!" he called, in a low voice. "I think the men are gone, but we must still be careful. Slowly and carefully take off the weed and shake yourselves free of the sand. Be ready to lie still at once if I say so."

But there was no need to say so—the men did not come back to the beach. The three children shook off the damp sand, threw the seaweed over the places where they had been lying and ran quickly to the shelter of the cliff, where no one could see them, if they looked over.

The gulls flew off in the greatest surprise and alarm. They could not understand rocks turning into children so suddenly. The young gull made up its mind that it would never land on a rock again—just suppose it changed into a person!

"Golly!" said Andy, as they stood shivering under the cliff. "That was a narrow escape! One man very nearly trod on my hand under the sand!"

"What have you done to your knee, Andy?" asked Jill, pointing to where Andy's knee was bleeding.

"A gull pecked me there," said Andy, mopping his knee. "It's nothing much. I say, wasn't it funny when the gulls thought we were rocks and came and stood on us! They were a great help!"

"One gull stood nearly on my face," said Jill. "I didn't like it very much."

"I do feel cold," said Mary, shivering and shaking. "It was horrid to be covered with damp sand for so long."

She sneezed. Andy looked at her anxiously. It would never do for any of them to be ill just now. He made up his mind quickly.

"The men may be off the island now," he said. "I'll go and see. If they are we'll all tear across to the hut, light the stove inside and dry ourselves. We'll make some hot cocoa and get really warm."

The girls thought that was a splendid idea. Andy set off up the cliff. "Stay here till you hear my seagull cry," he said. "Then come as quickly as you can."

He came to the top of the cliff. Then, keeping to the thick bracken, he made his way to the other side of the island, looking out for any signs of the men. He went right across the island, and came to the hollow where the old buildings were—and he saw the motor-boat putting off from the shore! The men had given up the hunt and were going back to the third island. They had already searched the second one and had found nobody but Tom.

Andy tore back to the girls. He screeched like a gull. The girls at once climbed the cliff and ran across the island, feeling a little warmer as they ran. Andy was in the shack, and the stove was lighted. It gave out a welcome heat.

"Take off your damp things and wrap yourself in the rugs," said Andy, who was already walking about in a rug himself and looked like a Red Indian. "I'm making some cocoa."

In ten minutes' time all the children felt warm and lively. The stove dried their things, and the hot cocoa warmed them well. Nobody sneezed again and Andy began to hope that their long stay under the damp sand wouldn't give anyone a chill after all.

"Andy, what are you going to do now?" asked Jill, sipping her cocoa. "We've got plenty of food, luckily, because we buried it all in the sand at the top of the beach out there—but we can't get away, because our boat's gone and we've lost Tom. Have we got to stay here for the rest of our lives?"

"Don't be silly, Jill," said Andy. "Let's tackle one thing at a time, for goodness' sake. We've done the most important thing so far—hidden ourselves so well that

we weren't found — and now we'll do the next most important thing — we'll rescue Tom! After that we'll think how to escape — but one thing at a time, please, and no worrying about what's going to happen. If we get worried, we'll get frightened, and nobody is any use when they're frightened. We've all got plenty of courage and we'll use it!"

Jill and Mary cheered up at Andy's brave words. "I *would* like to rescue poor Tom," said Jill. "He will be so lonely and upset. Where do you suppose he is?"

"In the cave where he left his camera, I expect," said Andy, pouring himself out another cup of cocoa. "And I'm pretty certain there'll be a guard somewhere at the entrance, for if there were not Tom would soon escape — so we won't run into trouble — we'll see if there isn't some other way of rescuing Tom."

"But how can there be?" asked Jill.

"I don't know yet," said Andy. "But I do know this — we thought it was impossible to hide safely on this bare little island — yet we did it! And so, though it sounds impossible to rescue Tom, there may be a way if we think hard enough. So now — let's all think hard!"

XVI

AN EXCITING DISCOVERY

Nobody could think how to rescue Tom. After all, if there was someone guarding the cave-entrance, how could Andy possibly get in without being seen?

The boy gave it up after a time, and for a change he set the gramophone going. There was only one record that was not broken, and that was the one with the lullaby on one side and the nursery rhymes on the other. The girls listened, rather bored, for they had heard that record scores of times since they had come to the island.

"Turn it off, Andy," said Jill. "If I hear that voice crooning that lullaby any more I shall go to sleep!"

Andy switched off the gramophone and went to the doorway of the shack. He was not afraid of the men coming back again for he was sure they thought there was no one on *this* island, at any rate.

A thought came into Andy's head. He went back to the girls.

"I think it would be a good thing if I crossed to the second island tonight, when it's dark," he said. "I might be able to get into touch with Tom somehow and hear what has happened, even if I can't rescue him."

"Oh, Andy—we shall be left all alone," said Mary in dismay.

"*We* don't mind that, if Andy can help Tom," said Jill. "We'll stay here in the hut, Andy, and try to sleep whilst you go. But do be careful, won't you?"

"I'll be careful," said Andy. "I don't want to be made

111

a prisoner, too—but you needn't be afraid of that! No enemy can catch *me*!"

So that night, when he had only the starlight to guide him, for the moon was not up, Andy crossed the line of rocks to the second island. He went very cautiously, for he did not want a single sound to come to the ears of anyone on the cave-beach.

He waded through the shallow water to the sand at the nearer end of the beach. He stood there, listening—and not very far off, close against the cliff where the cave-entrance was, he heard a cough!

"Oho!" said Andy to himself. "Thanks for that cough, dear sentry! I now know exactly where you are. You are behind the big rock at the cave opening. Well, I shall not go near you!"

The boy stood quite still for a while, listening. The sentry most obligingly cleared his throat and coughed again very loudly. Andy grinned. He made his way carefully round the end of the cliff and then began to climb up, feeling his way cautiously. The cliff there was not very steep, and Andy was soon at the top. He had not made a single sound.

He found a little hollow where heather and gorse grew thickly. He crept under an overhanging piece of bush, piled the heather beneath him, and slept peacefully. He knew he could do nothing till morning came, and he could see where he was.

The sun rose and Andy awoke. He was stiff and he stretched himself and yawned. He was hungry, but there was nothing for him to eat but bilberries.

He wriggled carefully to the edge of the cliff and looked over. Almost below him was the sentry he had heard last night, behind a rock at the cave-entrance. As

Andy looked down he saw a boat coming to the shore, and a man stepped off, and walked up the beach to change places with the sentry. They stood talking for a while and then the first sentry went to the boat, yawning, and the new one settled down to his task of waiting and watching.

Andy sat and thought. He wriggled back to a place where he imagined he must be exactly over the Round Cave. He wondered if Tom could hear him, if he drummed on the ground with his feet. After all, the boy could not be very far below, for the Round Cave was fairly high up in the cliff.

And then a most extraordinary thing happened — so startling that Andy's heart jumped almost out of his body!

A groan came from somewhere under his legs! Andy was lying on the heather, and when the groan came, he shot his legs up beneath him and stared at the place where the groan had come from as if he simply couldn't believe his eyes or ears!

A smaller groan sounded, more like a long yawn. Andy stared at the heather, and wondered if his ears could be right! Heather couldn't yawn or groan! Then what was it?

Very cautiously and gently, the boy turned himself about and began to feel in the heather. He pulled it to one side, and to his enormous astonishment he found a hole below the roots of the heather — a hole that must lead down to the Round Cave for Andy reckoned that he must be exactly over that cave.

Andy felt so excited that he began to tremble. "No wonder that cave didn't smell as musty and stuffy as we expected it to," he thought. "There is an air-hole leading

113

right down to it! Golly! I wonder if there's any chance of rescuing Tom this way."

He pulled up the heather and examined the hole. The earth was dry and sandy. Andy scraped away hard, and found that it was quite easy to make it bigger. Just suppose he could make it big enough to get down — or for Tom to get up!

"I knew there'd be a way if we didn't give up hope!" thought the excited boy. "I just knew it!"

He crawled to the top of the cliff and looked over it. The sentry was there still, and he was busy eating his breakfast. He was all right for some time.

Andy crawled back to the hole. He scraped about a little more, and then lay down with his face in the hole. It seemed to go down and down into the darkness.

Andy spoke in a low voice. "Tom! Are you there?"

And was Tom there? Yes, he was! He had been in the Round Cave, alone and lonely, ever since he had been caught. It had seemed ages to him. The boy had worried dreadfully about the others. He had eaten a little of the food around him, but he had no appetite now. He was miserable and frightened, though he would not show this to any of the sentries who occasionally came up the rocky passage-way to see if he was all right.

The man who could speak English had come to see him the evening before.

"We have searched the first island and this one," he had told Tom. "We have found your shack — and we have found your friends, too!"

Tom's heart sank when he heard this. The man was really telling an untruth, hoping to trap Tom into saying something that would show him there *were* others to be found. But Tom said nothing.

"I tell you we have found your friends," said the man. "They fought hard but they have been captured."

Tom stared at the man in surprise. He knew quite well that the girls would not fight men. What did this man mean? Could he be telling an untruth?

Then Tom suddenly knew that the man was hoping to trap him into saying something about the others. This man did not know that the "others" were only two girls and a boy. He did not even know for certain that there *were* any others!

"Well, two can play at a game of pretend like that!" thought the boy. So he put on a face of great surprise and said:

"Golly! *Are* there others on these islands then? I wish I'd known! I could have asked them for help!"

The man looked surprised. So perhaps this boy had no friends then? Could it be that he was really alone? The man did not know what to think. He said no more but turned and went out of the cave. Tom couldn't help feeling pleased. The man had thought he might trap him—but he felt sure *he* had tricked the man!

It was very lonely in the Round Cave. Tom slept heavily all the night through, but found the day very, very dull.

He sat on a box and groaned deeply. Then he yawned loudly. He was bored. He was lonely.

He sat there, doing nothing; and then he heard a very peculiar noise above his head—a kind of scraping noise. Tom wondered what it could be.

"Perhaps it's a rabbit or something," he thought. "But no—it couldn't be. The roof of the cave is of rock."

The scraping noise went on—and then something happened that made Tom leap up in fright.

A strange hollow voice came into the cave from somewhere! It ran all round the cave and Tom could just make out the words. The funny deep voice said, "Tom! Are you there?"

It was really Andy's voice, of course, coming down the hole to the cave—and the hole had made it sound deep and strange, not a bit like Andy's.

Tom trembled and said nothing. He couldn't understand this queer voice suddenly coming into the cave. So Andy spoke again.

"Tom! It's Andy speaking. Are you there?"

The voice rumbled round the cave—but this time Tom was not so scared. Could it really be Andy, somehow managing to speak to him? He answered as loudly as he dared.

"I'm here! In the Round Cave!"

Tom's voice came up to Andy, all muddled and jumbled, for Tom was not near the opening of the hole. Andy could not make out what he said, but he knew it was Tom speaking.

"Good!" he thought. "Tom's in there all right. I'll speak to him again and see if I can find out what's happened to him."

So once more Andy's voice came rumbling down into the cave. "Tom! I'm speaking down a hole that must somehow lead into your cave. See if you can find it and speak up it. I can't hear you properly. But whatever you do, don't let anyone hear you speaking to me."

Tom felt excited. Good old Andy! He got up and began to hunt around for the hole that led upwards to Andy. He must find it, he simply must!

XVII

A MARVELLOUS ESCAPE

Tom picked up the lamp and hunted around the cave. As he was doing this he heard the steps of the sentry coming up the rocky passage to the Round Cave. At once Tom sat down and began to sing loudly the lullaby that was on the unbroken gramophone record.

"Hush! Hush! Hush! You mustn't say a word! It's time for hush-a-bye, My little sleepy bird!"

These were the words of the rather silly lullaby song on the record. But they did very well indeed for a warning to Andy not to say anything for a moment! The sentry heard the boy singing, peeped in at him, said something that Tom didn't in the least understand, and went out again. He seemed surprised that the boy should sing. Tom went on singing the lullaby for a long time till he felt quite sure the sentry was not coming back.

Then he stopped singing and hurriedly began to hunt for the hole again. It didn't seem to be anywhere! The roof of the cave was not very high, and by standing on boxes and tins Tom could examine nearly every inch of it. But he could not find a hole that led upwards.

Andy's voice came booming down again: "Tom! Have you found the hole?"

The voice was so near Tom's ear that the boy nearly fell off the box he was standing on. He held up the lamp to the place where the voice came from. It was at the point where roof and wall met, at the back. The roof was of rock—but the wall just there was only of sand. Tom put his hand up and felt a cold draught blowing down the hole.

"Andy! I've found the hole!" he said, putting his head to it. "I say—tell me what's happened."

In low voices the two boys told one another all that had happened. Tom was very excited when he heard how the others had pretended to be seaweed-covered rocks.

"I *won*dered how you would hide," he said. "I couldn't *think* what you would do! Oh, Andy, I'm glad you're safe."

"Well, Tom, the next thing to do is to rescue *you*," said Andy. "I'm wondering if we can use this hole. What's it like at your end?"

"Rather small," said Tom. "I couldn't get up it unless I could make it larger. What's it like at your end?"

"I can easily make it as large as I like by scraping at it," said Andy. "Can you make your end large, too, do you think?"

Tom scraped at it with his hands. He could easily scrape the wall away, but not the roof. "I might perhaps be able to," he said. "But I'd want something to do it with—I've nothing but my hands."

"I've nothing but my hands either," said Andy, "and they are bleeding already from scraping at the soil. Listen, Tom—I shall go back to the girls soon, when the rocks are uncovered, but I can't wait till night. I must go now whilst the tide is low. So I want you to call to the sentry and pretend that you want his help in undoing a tin of food or something. See? Then whilst he is in the cave with you, I'll creep over the rocks safely without being seen, and get back."

"All right," said Tom. "What will you do then?"

"I'll collect something for us to work at the soil with,"

118

said Andy. "And I'll bring it back tonight. Then maybe we can make the hole large enough for you to crawl up. I don't think it's more than about six feet long. Now, wait to hear my seagull call, Tom — then yell for the sentry, and I'll make a dash for the rocks as soon as I see him go into the cave."

Everything worked well. When Tom heard Andy's seagull cry he shouted for the sentry, and the man went into the cave to see what was the matter.

He found that Tom had got a large tin of tongue, and seemed to have lost the tin-opener. The sentry hadn't one either, and he spent a very long time trying to open the tin with his pocket-knife. He ended in cutting his thumb very badly, and Tom produced a handkerchief and spent a long time binding up the man's thumb, glad to keep him in the cave so long.

Andy had plenty of time to escape back over the rocks. He knew them well now, and leapt from rock to rock easily. He was back in the shack in no time, it seemed!

The girls were thrilled to see him and he had to sit and tell them all he had done at least four or five times. When they heard about the hole leading down to the Round Cave the girls were tremendously excited.

"So you see," finished Andy, "I plan to get Tom out that way tonight — and I must take back with me something to dig and scrape with."

"Here's an old bit of wood with some jolly big nails in it, all sticking out," said Jill. "Would that do?"

"Yes — that's fine," said Andy. "Is there a bit for Tom?"

They found an old bit that would do. And then Andy said such a funny thing.

"I'll take the gramophone too! And the one record!"

The girls stared at him. "The *gram*ophone!" said Jill

at last. "Whatever for? Are you mad?"

"It does sound rather mad, I know," said Andy. "But I want it for something. I'll tell you afterwards. It won't sound quite so mad then!"

Andy had a very good meal, for he was awfully hungry. Then he settled down to sleep, for, as he said, he would not have much of a night *that* night!

The next night, after midnight, the boy went over the rocks again, carrying the pieces of rough wood with nails in, and the gramophone slung carefully over his shoulder. He reached the shore safely and made his way cautiously up the cliff.

And very soon Tom, half asleep, heard the queer hollow voice rumbling round his cave once more. "Tom! Are you asleep?"

Tom climbed on the chest and put his head to the hole. "Hallo, Andy!" he said. "I'm not asleep. I've been waiting and waiting for you!"

"There's a bit of wood with nails in coming down the hole," said Andy. "Scrape at your end with it and try your best to make the hole larger. I've got one too. I'll scrape my end. Look out that you don't get your eyes full of bits falling down."

The two boys set to work. Both of them scraped and dug for all they were worth. The soil was very dry and sandy, and was easy to move. Heaps of it fell down to Tom's end and he had to dodge it every now and again.

At last Andy's hole was quite big enough to get into. He called softly to Tom, "How are you getting on? My end is big enough for you to get out. I've got a rope I can let down to you if you are ready."

"I'm nearly ready," answered Tom, scraping hard. "Just a minute or two more!"

120

And then, at last, his end was large enough to climb into! The boy put another chest on the top of the one he was standing on and knelt upon it. His head and shoulders were right in the hole — he stood up and almost disappeared in the long narrow funnel.

"Wait a minute, Tom," said Andy. "I've got something I want to let down on the rope. It's the gramophone."

"The what?" asked Tom, in astonishment, thinking he couldn't have heard aright.

"The gramophone," said Andy. "I'm afraid, Tom, you may make rather a noise climbing down the cliff, and the sentry might think you had escaped — but if I

121

set the gramophone going, singing that silly lullaby you sang yesterday, he will think it's you still in the cave—and he won't come and see what the matter is. So I'm going to let it down, and you must set it right, and tie a bit of string to it so that I can pull the switch and set the record going when I think it's best to."

"Golly!" said Tom. "You think of everything!" The gramophone came bumping down the hole, on the end of the rope. Tom put it carefully behind a big chest and set the needle ready on the outside edge of the record. He tied a long piece of string to the starting-switch, and then tied the other end to the rope that Andy had let down with the gramophone.

"Pull it up, Andy," he said. "But carefully, please, because the string's on the rope and we don't want to break the needle by jerking the string too hard!"

Andy drew up the rope, untied the string on the end of it, and tied it to a heavy stone for safety. Then he called to Tom. "That's done. Come along up now, Tom. Don't brush against the gramophone string more than you can help. Here's the rope. Tie it round your waist and I'll help you up the hole by pulling—and I say, *don't* forget your camera!"

Tom stood up on the highest chest and began to scramble up the hole. There were plenty of rough ledges each side where he could put his feet. Andy hauled strongly on the rope, and Tom's head suddenly appeared through the hole by Andy's feet!

"Good!" said Andy. "Climb out!"

Tom climbed out. He sniffed the fresh breeze with delight, for it had ben rather stuffy down in the cave. Andy undid the rope from round Tom's waist. "Now you must get down the cliff as best you can without noise," he said. "Wait for me at the edge of the rocks, won't you. I'll give you a hand over those because I know them better than you do now."

Tom went to the cliff and began to climb down. Halfway down he slipped, and kicked out quickly to prevent himself from falling. A whole shower of stones fell down the cliff. The sentry, half-dozing, shouted at once.

Andy knew it was time to pull the string that was tied to the gramophone! He jerked it. The switch slid to one side and the record began to go round on its disc. The needle ran over the record and the lullaby began to sound in the cave. "Hush! Hush! Hush!"

The sentry heard it and thought it was Tom singing. He felt satisfied that his prisoner was still in the cave, as the song went on, and settled himself down again in a comfortable position. It must have been a rabbit that sent stones down the cliff, he thought!

Andy slipped down the cliff after Tom, glad that the sentry had heard the lullaby and had thought it must be Tom. Tom was waiting for him by the line of rocks.

"Didn't I make a row?" he whispered. "But I couldn't help it."

"It's all right! I set the record going and the sentry thinks you are busy in the cave, singing yourself to sleep," said Andy with a low chuckle. "Come on— we've no time to lose!"

XVIII

HEAVE-HO! HEAVE-HO!

Over the line of rocks the boys slipped and climbed,
Tom following Andy closely, for Andy now knew the
best way very well indeed. Big waves wetted them, but
they did not care. All they wanted was to get back to the
girls safely.

"The sentry won't look in at me tonight, I'm sure,"
said Tom, as they at last reached the sandy shore of the
beach. "And the one that comes in the morning may
not go into the cave to see me at all—he is a surly fellow."

"Well—that gives us a little time to think what to do
next," said Andy. "Though I'm blessed if I know what
will be best to do!"

They made their way to the shack, which was in
darkness, for Andy had forbidden the girls to show a
light of any sort in case the enemy saw it. Mary and
Jill were lying together on their heather bed in the
darkness, fast asleep.

Mary heard the boys come in and she sat upright in
bed at once. "Is that you, Andy?"

"Yes—and Tom too!" said Andy. Jill awoke then,
and the four of them sat on one bed, hugging one another
for joy. Now they were all together again! It was lovely.

"I was an awful idiot to try and get my camera back,"
said Tom. "I never thought of being caught. Now our
boat is gone and it's going to be difficult to know what
to do."

"There's only one thing to do," said Andy. "And that

is to get our fishing-boat off the rocks early to-morrow morning somehow—and refloat her. I've noticed she seems to have moved a bit, and it may be that the tides have loosened her. Perhaps the two rocks that held her are not holding her quite so fast now. Anyway, it's our only chance."

"Yes—we'll try and do that," said Jill. "Tom's escape is sure to be discovered sometime to-morrow, and this time such a search will be made that I know we'll all be found."

"Well, let's sleep for an hour or two till dawn," said Andy. "We can't do anything at the moment."

So they all lay down on their beds and slept until Andy awakened them two hours later. Now dawn was in the sky and soon the sun would rise.

The children slipped across the island and came to the beach where they had first landed, after their wreck. They looked at their poor fishing-boat, still jammed between the rocks. Certainly it had moved a little—it was not leaning so much to one side.

They stood and looked at it. The tide was not very high yet, and it was possible to reach the boat without too much difficulty.

It was not long before all the children had reached their boat, and were clambering up the wet and slippery deck. Seaweed lay across it now, thrown there by the waves. The boat looked old and miserable—not at all like the smart little ship in which they had started out so gaily.

The boys went down into the little cabin. It had water lying at the bottom. Andy ripped up the planks and examined the boat underneath the floor of the cabin.

Then he came out and let himself down the side of the

ship, disappearing under the water to feel the bottom of the boat. The girls and Tom watched him anxiously.

"We *must* mend the boat somehow," said Tom. "It's our only chance!"

When Andy joined them on the slanting deck he looked very cheerful.

"Do you know, there's not much wrong!" he said. "I do believe I could patch her up fairly quickly. The waves have shifted her a bit so that I can get at the damaged part—the part where she struck the rocks and damaged a few planks."

"Oh, *good*, Andy!" cried the girls, and Tom slapped the fisher-boy on the shoulder for joy. How marvellous that they could perhaps make the ship seaworthy again! What luck that the waves had shifted her enough to make it possible to examine the damaged part! Tom had no idea at all how Andy meant to patch up the ship, but he meant to help with all his might, to make up for losing the stolen boat.

Tom and Andy went back over the rocks to fetch a rope. Andy felt sure that if they all tugged at the boat at high tide, they could get her off the rocks and float her to the beach, where it would not be difficult to patch her up.

"You see, Tom, she's not jammed very tightly now," said Andy. "And I reckon if we wait till the tide is at its very highest, and big waves are trying to lift the boat up, we could pull her right off the rocks! Then we'll get her into shore somehow, and see what we can do."

"If only we can do it all before the enemy come again," said Tom. "I wonder if they've discovered that I've gone!"

"Don't let's think about that," said Andy.

The boys found all the rope they had and wound it

firmly round their waists. They went back to the shore. The girls were still on the ship, but the tide was rising high and they would soon have to leave, as the sea covered the boat at high tide.

The children fastened strong double strands of rope to the front of the ship. Then, holding firmly to the rope, they clambered over the rocks back to the sandy beach, wet through. The tide came up higher and higher and the children had to stand up to their waists in the water, for the rope would not reach right to the shore.

"Look! There's an enormous wave coming!" shouted Andy. "Pull on the rope, all of you, as soon as the wave strikes the ship! *Heave*-ho!"

They all pulled—and every child felt the ship give a little as the wave lifted her and the rope pulled her. "Now here's another one!" yelled Andy. "*Heave*-ho!"

They all heaved at the rope with all their might. Again they felt the ship move a little. The two big waves ran up the shore and wetted the children to their chins!

"Hang on to the rope, girls," cried Andy. "If we get many waves like that you may be swept off your feet. But as long as you've got hold of the rope you'll be all right."

The waves were smaller after that—and then the wind began to blow stiffly again, and the waves grew bigger. An enormous one reared its green head far out to sea.

"There's a monster coming!" shouted Tom. "Look at it! It will sweep us off our feet!"

"But we'll pull at the boat first!" yelled Andy, who was tremendously excited. He really felt that they could get the boat off the rocks. "Now—*heave*-ho, *heave*-ho!"

The wave struck the boat and the rope dragged at her at the same moment. She shivered and groaned as she

127

tried to escape from the rocks that held her. She slipped a few feet forward.

The giant wave struck the children next, and all of them went down under it, even Andy. They floundered in the foaming waves, and Jill swallowed about a pint of salt water. Mary was very angry because Tom put his foot into her neck, but Tom didn't mean to. The wave struck him so hard that he was flung right off his feet, and had to strike out to get himself upright again.

None of them let go the rope. They all held on for dear life, as Andy had ordered. So it was not long before they were standing up again, gasping and spluttering, salt in their mouths and noses, but all of them determined to heave again as soon as the next big wave came.

"*Look* how the boat has moved!" yelled Andy, in the greatest delight. "She's almost off the rocks! Golly! Isn't this exciting?"

The boat had moved a good deal. Andy was sure that they could pull her in now. He waited patiently for the next big wave to come—and my goodness, it was a monster! The tide was at its height now, and the wind blew very strongly. A green wave put up its head, and the children gave a yell.

"Look at that one!"

"It will knock us all over again," said Mary, afraid. But she didn't let go the rope. Whether she was knocked over or not she meant to do her bit.

The wave grew bigger and higher as it came nearer to the rocks on which the boat lay. It began to curl over a little—and then it struck the rocks, and the boat too.

"HEAVE-HO!" yelled Andy, in a voice as enormous as the wave! And they all heaved. My goodness, what a heave that was!

The great wave blotted the boat from their sight and came raging towards them. Jill gave a shout of fear.

"Hold on!" shouted Andy, half-afraid himself. The wave swept them all off their feet—and alas, swept them all from the rope too, except Andy, who held on with all his might.

The other three children were taken like corks, rolled over and over, and flung roughly on the sand at the edge of the sea. Then the great wave ran back down the beach, gurgling and foaming.

Jill sat up, crying. Mary lay still, quite stunned for the moment. Tom sat up, furiously angry with the wave!

It had bumped and battered him most spitefully, he thought.

As for Andy, he was under water, still clinging to the rope — but as soon as he struggled to his feet he gave a gurgling shout and tried to clear his throat of the salt water there.

"The ship! Look! She's off and floating!"

They all looked — and there was the little fishing-boat, safely off the rocks, bobbing about on the sea that swirled high over the other rocks.

"Come in and help me, quick, before any other big waves come!" yelled Andy. "We can get her into shore now. Quick, Tom!"

The three battered children, dripping wet, ran bravely into the sea again. They caught hold of the rope and pulled hard. "*Heave*-ho, *heave*-ho, *heave*-ho!" chanted Andy, as they all pulled hard.

And the boat came bobbing in to the shore! The children dragged the rope up the beach and the boat followed, scraping its bottom at last on the sand.

"We've got her!" shouted Andy, doing a kind of war-dance on his tired legs. "We've got her! Now we'll just see what we can do!"

XIX

A SHOCK FOR THE CHILDREN

The four children were so excited at getting their boat off the rocks that at first they could do nothing but laugh and chatter and clap their hands. They were all tired out with their long struggle in the sea, but so happy that they forgot all about their aching arms and legs, salty mouths and dripping clothes.

The boat lay on her side in the shallow water. Andy examined her carefully. He was sure that if he could nail planks inside, just where she had been stove-in by the rocks, he could patch her up well enough for her to sail home.

"She will let water in, but you two girls can bail her out all the time," said Andy. "I'll patch her up enough to get her sailing safely. Golly! I never thought we could do this!"

The children had been so busy that no one, not even Tom, had thought of any breakfast. But Andy suddenly felt very hungry, and sent the girls off to fetch breakfast of some sort. "And bring a jug of hot cocoa, too," he said. "We are all wet through, and it would be nice to have something to warm us."

Tom fetched the tools from the shack and the box of nails and screws and bolts. Andy meant to be very busy indeed. Somehow or other that boat had to be finished before Tom's escape was known.

After a hurried breakfast, they all set to work under Andy's orders. Andy stripped some of the wood from the roof of the cabin to use in the patching of the ship. The girls took out the old nails from the strips. Tom waited on Andy and handed him everything he wanted.

The sound of the hammer echoed over the island. "Do you think the enemy will hear?" asked Jill anxiously.

"Can't help it if they do," said Andy. "We can't hammer without noise! Pass me the biggest nails you've got, Tom."

They all worked steadily for the whole of the morning. And at last Andy heaved a sigh of relief.

"Well—I think that's patched up. She won't last long without being bailed out, because I can't patch her really properly—but the girls can easily bail out whilst you and I sail the boat, Tom."

"Is she ready?" asked the girls eagerly.

"As ready as I can make her," said Andy. "Now you girls must go and get all the rugs, and Tom and I will get the food from where we buried it under the sand, at the top of our own beach by the shack. We'll pile in everything we can, push her out into the water and sail off! Golly, I never thought we'd be able to do this!"

The four of them set off to fetch everything. They felt cheerful and excited. It might take them ages to get home—but at last they were going to leave these strange unknown islands safely, and take their secret with them!

The girls gathered up the rugs. The boys tied the tins and boxes together and staggered over the island with their heavy load, back to the boat again.

It was difficult climbing down the cliff so heavily-laden, but they managed it safely. The girls threw down the rugs on the deck, and the boys packed the food into the cabin. Now they could go!

"Wait a bit—we'll take the old sail with us," said

132

Andy, "I could rig it again, and it would help us."

He set off to get the sail—and then he suddenly stopped and looked down on the beach. There, by his foot, lay something that greatly astonished him.

"What is it, Andy?" called Tom, seeing Andy's puzzled face.

"Look at this," said Andy, picking up a dry, clean match, that had already been struck.

"What about it? It's only a match," said Tom.

"It's a match that hasn't very long been struck," said Andy. "And it is lying on sand that has been covered and uncovered by the tide since we've been working on the boat this morning. Well—has any of *us* struck a match and thrown it down? No—we haven't! Then who has?"

"Oh, Andy—surely you are mistaken," said Jill, looking ready to cry. "Nobody else has been here. We should have seen them."

"I'm wondering if anyone has been here whilst we were fetching the rugs and the food," said Andy, looking all round. "I don't like it—and, oh golly—look at that set of footprints in the sand over there! They are not *our* footprints!"

The four children gazed at the set of large footprints. Whoever made them had been wearing nailed boots—and the children all wore rubber shoes.

The girls were frightened. Yes—someone had been on the beach whilst they had left it to get rugs and food. But who? And where was he?

"Well—let's get the boat launched and hope to get away before we're stopped," said Andy. "Come on—we'll do without the sail."

They ran to the boat and took hold of the rope to drag it down to the sea—but even as they took hold of it, a loud voice shouted to them from round the corner of the cliff.

"Stop! Halt!"

The children stopped hauling the boat and stared round. They saw the enemy—four of them! One of them was the man who spoke English, and it was he who was shouting.

The children stared in fright at the four men, who came quickly over the beach.

They spoke to one another in a foreign language. Then the first man spoke again.

"So! There are four of you—and all children! This is the boy who escaped—ah, you thought you were very clever, didn't you!"

"I did, rather," said Tom boldly. He *felt* frightened— but he wasn't going to show it! No—he was British, and these men shouldn't think they could scare *him*!

"You took your boat off the rocks, and thought you would escape safely, didn't you?" said the man mockingly. "Well, you made a mistake. We shall now take the boat away—and you shall remain prisoners on this island for as long as we want you to! Take out the food and the blankets again. You will need those if you live here for months!"

The children sulkily took out all the food and rugs they had so cheerfully put into the boat. Tom was glad to see that neither Jill nor Mary cried. Good! That would show the enemy how brave British children could be!

"Now we are going," said the man who spoke English. He gave a rapid order to the other men, who ran off round the cliff and then reappeared in a small boat, bobbing on the waves. It was plain that they had landed round the cliff, watched the children, and then come to catch them.

Andy and the others had to watch the men drag their ship down to the sea and launch it. They had tied their little rowing-boat behind it, and now, waving mockingly to the children, they made their way over the water, round the cliff, and out of sight, rowing Andy's boat along swiftly.

The children watched them go, anger and despair in their hearts. All their work for nothing! How they had battled with the sea that morning—how they had slaved to get that boat right! And now they had all been discovered, their boat had been taken, and they were real prisoners.

Andy shook his fist at the disappearing ship, with the small boat bobbing behind it.

"You think you can beat a Scots boy, but you can't," he cried. "I'll beat you yet! You and your submarines!"

Wearily the children gathered up the old rugs and all the food and made their way up the cliff, across the island and back to their shack. They packed the food on the floor in a corner and threw the rugs on the beds.

Then they sat on the beds and looked at one another. Not till then did the girls begin to cry. But cry they did, letting the tears run down their cheeks without trying to wipe them off. They were so tired and so disappointed.

Tears came into Tom's eyes too, when he saw the two miserable girls. But he blinked them back, after one look at Andy's lean brown face. Andy's blue eyes were like stones, and his mouth was stern and straight. Andy was not thinking of crying or grumbling. Andy was angry and fierce, and he sat in silence, looking straight before him, thinking hard.

"Andy — what are you thinking about?" asked Tom at last. "You look so stern. You're not angry with *us*, are you?"

"No," said Andy. "We all did our best — and we've got to do our best again. I tell you, Tom, we've *got* to leave this island! Somehow, we've got to get away and tell our secret. No matter what happens to any of us we must try to get home and tell all we have seen! As long as the enemy remain hidden in these islands, able to come here whenever they need food or fuel, then just so long will our ships be sunk round about these seas."

"Oh, Andy — it's all very well to say things like that — but how *can* we get away now our boat's gone?" said Jill, wiping her eyes.

"I'll think of a way," said Andy. "*Some*how, I'll think of a way. I'm going out by myself now, to puzzle a way out of this fix. Don't come with me. I want to be alone."

The boy slipped out of the shack. He climbed the cliff and sat in the heather by himself, his blue eyes fixed on the sky-line. How could he get home? How could he tell his secret? For two hours he sat there, puzzling and worried, so still that the gulls circled round his head and wondered if he were asleep.

And then Andy straightened himself and got up. He went down to the others, his eyes shining and his head up. "I've thought of a way," he said proudly. "I've thought of a way at last!"

XX

ANDY MAKES A PLAN

Tom, Mary and Jill looked at Andy, excited.

"Do you really know a way of escape, even now that our ship has been taken?" asked Jill. "You *are* clever, Andy."

"Well, it's no use us trying to take one of the enemy's boats again, or to get our own ship back," said Andy. "And it's no use putting up a signal to passing ships, for two reasons—one is that I am perfectly certain no ship ever passes near these islands, or they would have discovered the secret of the submarines before this—and the second reason is that I am jolly sure the enemy wouldn't let us have a signal up anyhow!"

"Go on," said Tom, feeling sure Andy had got a very good idea coming.

"Well, my idea is—we'd better make a raft!" said Andy. "We can't get a boat or make one—but we *could* make a rough kind of raft, and get a mast of some sort to rig a sail on. We've plenty of food to take with us—and you and I, Tom, could set off alone on it to try and make for home. I daren't take the girls—they would be so cold on an open raft, and they would be safer here."

"Not take *us!*" cried Jill indignantly. "Of *course* you'll take us! We won't be left behind—will we, Mary?"

"Listen, Jill—you're only ten years old and not very big," said Andy patiently. "If we take you it will make things much more difficult for Tom and for me. If we get home safely we can have you rescued at once—

if we don't get home you will at least be safe on the island."

The girls cried bitterly at this. They thought it was very unfair. They couldn't know that Andy didn't feel at all certain of ever getting home, and was very much afraid of the girls being washed overboard when big waves came. He and Tom were strong—and besides they were boys—but the girls would never be able to stand tossing about on a raft for days and days.

Andy was quite firm about it, and the girls dried their eyes and listened to his plans. Tom wondered what the raft was to be made of.

"We shall have to pull our wooden hut to pieces and use the planks," said Andy. "Luckily we've got plenty of nails to use."

"But what shall we live in if we pull down the shack?" asked Jill in dismay.

"I've thought of that," said Andy. "You see, if we start pulling down the shack the enemy are bound to notice it and will guess what we are doing. Well—I thought we could make it look as if our hut had fallen down on us, and I could ask the enemy to give us a tent to live in instead. Then we could live in that, and quietly make our raft from the fallen-down shack!"

"That really *is* a good idea," said Tom. "We get the two things we want—somewhere else to live—and wood to make a raft—and the enemy actually help us without knowing it!"

"Yes," said Andy, grinning round at the other three. "We'd better wait a day or two, though, because the enemy are bound to watch us a bit at first, to see if we've any other ideas of escape. We won't do anything suspicious at all for the next few days."

"All right," said the others, and they began to feel excited again. They still felt terribly disappointed when they thought of how their precious boat had been taken from them—but never mind, perhaps their raft would be luckier.

So for the next few days the children just played about, bathing, fishing, paddling, and the enemy, who sent a man over every day at noon, saw nothing to make him think that the children had any plans at all.

"I think there's going to be a storm," said Andy, on the third evening. "That would be a good reason for our shack to fall down, I think! As soon as that man has come and gone today we'll turn the shack into a ruin!"

The man came, looked round the island and went. As soon as he had gone the children set about the hut. Andy removed nails and took out planks. He hammered part of the roof away and made a big hole. He made one side of the hut so weak that it fell in on top of the girls' bed.

"Doesn't it look a ruin now!" said Jill, with a giggle. "We'd better spread the sail over that side of the hut, Andy, or the rain will come in tonight."

"Yes, we'll do that," said Andy. So when they had done all they could to make the hut look as if it was falling to pieces, they draped the sail over the open side for protection, and then grinned at one another.

"And to-morrow we will act a nice little play for the enemy!" said Andy with a chuckle. "We will pretend that in the storm which we can now hear rumbling round, our hut was blown in—and we will bandage up Jill's head as if the hut fell on top of her—and bandage my leg too. And we'll beg for a tent most humbly!"

"I hope I shan't giggle," said Mary.

"If you do you'll deserve a good slapping," began

139

Andy fiercely—but Mary spoke hastily once more.

"I didn't mean it, Andy. I *shan't* giggle. I shall be frightened, really, though I won't show it."

"All right," said Andy, calming down. "Golly! What a loud clap of thunder!"

The storm began properly then. It was not a very bad one, but the children were glad of the protection of the big sail over the open side of the hut. The wind blew fiercely, and Andy and Tom had to weight the sail down to prevent it from being blown away. The thunder rumbled and crashed and the lightning flickered round the islands. In an hour's time, however, the storm was gone, and the wind died down again.

In the morning the children took the sail and hid it safely, for Andy did not want the enemy to know he had an old sail. They made the shack look as if the wind had almost blown it down, and Jill broke a plate and threw the pieces about as if the storm had caused the accident.

"Now I'll tie up Jill's head in my big handkerchief," said Andy, taking out a rather dirty hanky. "And I'll use a rag to tie my leg up with. We'll pretend we got hurt in the night."

When the man came to look at the children and go over the island as usual, he was surprised to find Jill bandaged up, and Andy limping.

Andy hailed him. "Hie! Our shack has fallen down! Come and see!"

The man went to look. He could not speak English, but he understood at once that the shack had fallen down on the children during the storm. Jill sat on the ground, pretending to cry, holding her head in her hand. Mary was trying to comfort her.

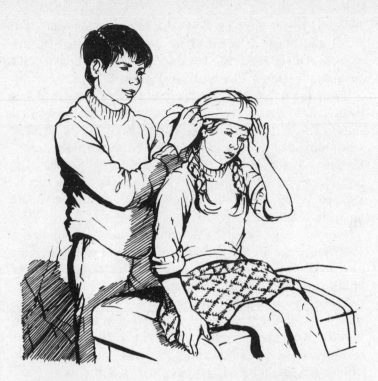

"We want a tent to sleep in," said Andy. The man did not understand. Tom took out his notebook and drew a tent in it. Then the man understood. He nodded his head, said something that sounded like "Yah, yah!" to the children, and set off in his boat.

"Don't cry too much, Jill, or the man will want to see your wound!" said Andy. "I was awfully afraid he would take off the bandage and have a look to see how much your head was hurt."

"Gracious!" said Jill, in alarm. "I didn't think of that!"

"I hope he comes back with a tent," said Tom. "You'd better go up the cliff, Jill, and sit on the top, so that if the man comes back he won't ask to see your head."

Jill and Mary went off. Tom and Andy waited for the man to return. He came back in about three hours—and he brought a tent! The boys were pleased.

The man looked round for the girls. He touched his head, and looked at Andy. He was trying to say he wanted to see the girl with the bandaged head. Andy nodded and pointed to the top of the cliff. "She's all right now," he said. The man saw the girls sitting up on the cliff and seemed satisfied. He put the tent down on the beach, showed Andy the ropes and pegs with it and went off again in his boat.

"Good!" said Andy. "We'll put this tent up in a sheltered place in the next cove. We don't want the man visiting this hollow too often, or he may notice that the shack is gradually disappearing!"

They put up the tent in the next cove, just around the cliff, in as sheltered a place as possible at the end of the beach where heather grew thickly, and big cushions of thrift were soft and plentiful. They made themselves beds of heather and bracken and piled the rugs there.

The man came again next day and Andy showed him where they had put the tent. Andy limped about with the rag still on his leg, which made the others want to smile—but the man did not once guess that it was all pretence. As soon as he had gone Andy walked and ran just as usual!

The weather was not so good now. The sun was not so warm, and clouds sailed over the sky, bringing showers of rain at times. The children often had to sit in the tent, and they longed to begin making the raft.

"I don't want to start it till I'm sure the man has forgotten about the tumble-down shack," said Andy.

142

"Yesterday he brought his boat in to this beach instead of the next one, and hardly looked over the island at all. If he comes to this cove today, we can begin the raft this afternoon."

The man came at noon as usual. This time he brought a large supply of food, and tried to make the children understand that he would not be back for a few days. He pointed to three fingers and shook his head.

"I think he means he won't be back for three days," said Andy, his heart jumping for joy. He nodded to the man, who, instead of looking over the island as he usually did, got straight back into his boat and rowed off.

"Well, if that isn't a bit of luck!" said Andy joyfully, as soon as he had gone. "I'm sure he won't be back for some days — *and* he's brought us a marvellous supply of food, that will just do beautifully for the raft! We can safely begin building it this afternoon!"

XXI

THE BUILDING OF THE RAFT

The four children tackled the shack that afternoon and tore out as many planks as they could.

"Pile them up in different sizes," ordered Andy. "Come and help with this long plank, Tom—it's too heavy for me to pull out alone."

By the end of that day the children had sixteen planks of different sizes piled up. Andy was pleased.

"If we can get as many as that to-morrow, we'll be able to make a really fine raft," he said. "Tom, you are saving all those long screws and nails, aren't you? We shall need them soon."

"Yes—they're all safe," said Tom, showing Andy a tin into which he had put all the screws and nails he had taken out of the planks.

"Do you think we'd better hide these planks in case the man *does* come to-morrow, although we feel sure he won't?" asked Jill.

"Well—perhaps we had better," said Andy, who was feeling tired and not at all eager to carry heavy planks about. So he and Tom took the planks one by one and hid them in thick heather. Then they went to have a good meal, which the girls had been getting ready.

"I've never been so hungry in my life!" said Tom.

"You've said that about a thousand times since we've been on this island," said Jill. "Well—see if you can eat *that* plateful!"

Tom took the plate. It was full of cold tongue, baked

potatoes, and tinned asparagus tips which the man had brought yesterday. There were also sliced pears, tinned milk to eat with them, and hot cocoa. The pears and tinned milk were so delicious that Tom wanted a second helping.

"Good gracious! At the rate you eat you'll want about a thousand tins on the raft!" said Mary, opening another tin of pears. "Andy, I hope you won't forget to take a tin-opener when you go. It would be so awful to be hungry, and have heaps of tinned food round you—and not be able to eat any of it because you had forgotten an opener!"

Andy grinned. "I shan't forget *that*," he said. "Golly, I *am* tired!"

They were all tired, and they fell asleep in the tent almost as soon as they lay down on their heathery beds. They awoke late the next day and Andy could not make up his mind whether to get on with the raft or not.

"I'm pretty sure that fellow meant he wouldn't come for a few days," Andy said. "But if he *did* happen to come and found us at work on a raft, it would be *too* disappointing for anything."

"Well, one of us could go up to the rocky ledge and keep watch all the time, couldn't we," said Jill eagerly. "We could easily see anyone coming, then, and give warning in time to let you and Tom hide everything."

"Yes—of course," said Andy. "That's a good idea! Take it in turns of about two hours each. You go first, Jill, and Mary next."

So Jill went up to the rocky ledge and sat there. She could see the cave-beach of the next island and had a good view of any boat that might come over the water.

No boat was to be seen—but all that day the islands

were very noisy indeed! Seaplanes flew over many times, their engines roaring loudly. Three came down in the calm water opposite the cave-beach. Jill watched them carefully.

Stores were taken to the cave, as she could plainly see. The seaplanes roared away after a time—but all that day others flew over the islands, and the children wondered to see so many.

"Well, there's one thing that's lucky," said Andy with a grin. "Those seaplanes make such a noise that no one could possibly hear the sound of any hammering today —so I vote we get on with it and make as much noise as we like now there's a chance!"

So the sound of hammering was heard on the children's island that day, as Andy and Tom nailed twelve big planks crosswise to twelve others below. Then on top of the two crosswise rows Andy nailed yet another row of shorter planks to make the raft really solid and heavy.

The boys added a kind of rim to the raft to prevent things rolling off too easily. Andy was clever at carpentry and he knew all the best tricks of making each plank hold the other fast. It was a very solid-looking affair that began to take shape by the time that night came.

Andy had found a strong post that would do for a mast, but he did not mean to put this up till the raft was almost ready to launch. "We can't very well hide a raft with a mast," he said. "It is easier to hide a flat raft with no mast, if that man pays us a visit too soon."

"How can we hide it, though?" asked Tom, looking at the heavy raft. "We really can't toss it lightly into the heather as we could do with planks!"

Andy grinned. "We'll hide it in a very easy place," he said. "We'll simply rig up the tent above it, and pile heather on the raft, which will then make the floor. I don't think anyone is likely to think that our tent hides a raft!"

In three days the raft was quite complete, and was very sound and solid. Andy had decided to take all the food in the big wooden box in which the man had brought the tins and jars on his last visit.

"We can nail the box to the floor of the raft," said Andy, "and our food will stay there quite safely! If we put it loose on the deck of the raft, everything would get thrown off in a rough sea, even though we've put a kind of rail to the edge of the raft."

There came a warning cry from Jill not long after that. She had seen a boat coming round the cliff on the far side of the cave-beach. Hastily the boys put up the tent over the raft, and Mary strewed the heather and bracken over the deck. She could not hide the box of food in the middle of the raft, however.

"Never mind about that," said Andy. "Put a rug over it, and it will look like a seat or something."

There were two men this time, and one of them was the one who spoke English.

The boat drew up in the cove where the raft was, and one man got out. It was not the man who had seen the fallen-down shack, but the one who spoke English.

Andy went down to meet him. "Please, sir, won't you give us a boat to go home in?" asked Andy, knowing perfectly well that the man would say no.

"No," said the man at once. "You will stay here for as long as we wish. But soon the winter will come, and a tent will be no good to you. Is there any building here that can be mended?"

"No," said Andy, who did not wish the man to examine the buildings, and perhaps ask where the tumbledown shack was. This had almost disappeared by now, for the children had taken all the planks for their raft!

"Let me see your tent," said the man. Andy's heart sank. It would be too bad if the raft was found just as it was finished. He took the man to the tent in silence.

The man looked inside. He saw the box in the middle covered with a rug. "What's that?" he asked.

"It's the box of food the man brought us the other day," said Andy, and he pulled off the rug. The man saw at once that it *was* only a box of food and he nodded. He did not go inside the tent, luckily, or his nailed boot might have gone through the heathery covering and struck against the wooden raft below. Then he would certainly have pulled aside the heather and seen the children's secret.

Jill and Mary watched, very pale and scared. Tom sat nearby and whistled. The man still stood looking into the tent, and all the children felt very anxious indeed — and then a great seaplane roared over the island, making a terrific noise.

"Look! Look!" yelled Tom, jumping up. "Isn't it a big one!"

The man looked up, at Tom's yell, and followed the seaplane with his eyes. "I must go," he said, and he went down the beach to the boat. "I will send men to put you up a rough hut for the winter. Be sensible children and you will be looked after — but if not, you will be very sorry for yourselves."

The children were very thankful indeed when they saw the boat go off over the water. They heaved deep sighs of relief and looked at one another.

"Thank goodness, that seaplane came when it did and Tom let out that yell," said Jill. "It just took the man's attention away! I really thought he was going to go inside the tent and look at everything!"

"Well, I think we're safe to make our escape soon now," said Andy. "I don't expect any men will be sent for a while. We'll drag the raft down to the shore early to-morrow morning, and I'll set up the mast and rig the sail as best I can. Then Tom and I will start off."

The girls said nothing. They did not like being left alone on the island — and yet they knew that Andy was right. Somehow he must get home and tell the people there the secrets they had discovered. The raft would not really take four—and the girls were not strong enough to stand days and nights of tossing about on the sea.

"Well, Andy, it's very important that you should get back and tell the secret of these islands," said Jill at last. "So, for the sake of our country, Mary and I will stay behind here without any fuss and do the best we can, whilst you and Tom set off for home. But do rescue us as soon as possible!"

"Of course we shall," said Andy, glad to see that the girls were going to be brave and not make any fuss. "You are good sports, you two girls—I really do feel proud of you both—don't you, Tom?"

"*Very* proud," said Tom. And the girls went red with pleasure.

"We'll wish you luck to-morrow!" said Jill. "Oh, how I hope you'll soon get back home, Andy! Mary and I will watch every day till you come back."

They all went to bed early that night, for to-morrow was to be an important day! They did not sleep very well, for they were too excited.

And in the morning, early, they took down their tent, dragged off the heather that covered the raft, and tied ropes to it, to pull it down to the beach.

"Now we're off on another adventure!" said Andy, dragging the raft. "Heave-ho! Heave-ho! Down to the sea we go!"

XXII

AWAY ON THE SEA

The raft was dragged right down to the sea. In the middle of it Andy fixed the post that was to be the mast. He rigged up the old sail very cleverly. The box of food was firm below the mast — they had enough to last them for some days. They took a big tin of water with them too, but expected to use the juice of the tins of fruit to quench their thirst after they had drunk all the water.

Andy had made two rough paddles to help the boat along and to guide it. The girls handed the boys the two warmest rugs to wrap themselves in at night, though Andy said they wouldn't be any use — they would get wet with the very first wave that splashed over the raft! But to please the girls he took the rugs.

"Andy, you can dry them in the sun in the daytime," said Jill, "and you *might* be glad of them. Mary and I have got plenty here."

The raft was ready to float off at last. The boys gave the girls a hug and said good-bye.

"Now don't worry," said Andy, jumping on to the raft. "You won't hear for days and days, because we've got to get back home, and then tell our tale and then ships have got to find their way here. So you'll have to wait a long time."

"What shall we say if the enemy want to know where *you* are?" asked Jill anxiously.

"Just say we have disappeared," said Andy. "And if you like to do another bit of pretending and make a fuss — well, do it!"

"All right," said Jill. "Anyway, you may be quite sure we shan't tell them you've gone on a raft."

"No—we don't want their seaplanes hunting the sea for us!" said Andy, letting the sail unfurl. "Now—good-bye, Jill! Good-bye, Mary! See you soon!"

"Good-bye, Andy! Good-bye, Tom!" cried the girls, trying to smile cheerfully, though they felt very miserable and lonely to see the boys setting off together. "Good luck!"

Tom pushed out the raft and jumped up on it. He took a paddle and guided it. Andy let the sail billow out. The wind caught it and the little raft leapt along over the waves like a live thing!

"I say! It *can* get along, can't it!" cried Jill, jumping up and down in excitement. "Look how it bobs over the waves!"

The boys waved wildly to the girls. Little waves splashed over the deck of the raft and wetted the boys' legs. If they ran into a stormy sea they would soon be wet through—but at the moment they cared nothing for what might happen! They were very excited and very anxious to guide their little raft on the right course.

The sail flapped and billowed finely. Andy had rigged it most cleverly, and the wind shot the little craft along swiftly.

"It's going nearly as fast as the ship!" said Tom in delight.

"No—it isn't really," said Andy, shaking his head. "No raft could ever equal a boat for speed—it's so clumsy and heavy. But I must say our raft isn't bad! Look out —there's a fat wave coming!"

The raft sailed into the wave—slap! It drenched Tom, and he laughed and shook himself like a dog. The sun was out and the boy's clothes soon dried.

The boys looked back at the shore of their island, which now seemed far away. They could just make out the two girls, who had now climbed to the top of the cliff and were standing there, watching the raft out of sight.

"I hope Jill and Mary will be all right," said Tom. "Poor kids—it was awful having to leave them alone."

"Yes," said Andy. "But it was the only thing to be done. We've happened on very big things, Tom—and so we've got to be big enough and brave enough to meet them."

"Well—I'm not afraid," said Tom stoutly. "And as for you, Andy, I really don't believe anything in the world would frighten you!"

"Oh yes, it would," said Andy. "But I'd not show I was frightened! Look, Tom—you can see *all* the islands now!"

The boys stood on the raft, holding on to the mast and looked back on the cluster of islands. They lay in the sea together, and looked very small now that the boys were so far off. They could no longer see the girls. And soon even the islands too would disappear—then the boys would be quite alone on the wide sea.

"Do you really know which way to go, Andy?" said Tom.

"More or less," said Andy. "I can guide the raft by the sun in the day-time, and by the stars at night. It's a good thing for us that the wind is just in the right direction. I hope it lasts. It's easy enough now—but if the wind changes, things will be very difficult!"

Now the boys could no longer see any land at all. They were alone on the wide green sea. Below them the

153

water was very, very deep. The sea was not rough, but a little choppy, and the raft bobbed like a cork over the waves. Every now and again a wave hopped over the side and wetted the deck of the raft. The boys got used to this and didn't even move when a wave reared its head to run across the raft.

Tom dragged his hand in the cool water. He liked the movement of the raft running over the sea. The sun shone steadily down and the boys became very hot. Tom took off his jersey and hung it safely over the top of the mast, out of reach of the waves.

"Golly! I'm cooking!" he said. Luckily the boys had got hats with them, and these shaded the sun from their heads or they might have felt sick. The sun blazed down, and at last the boys let themselves drop into the sea, holding on to the edge of the raft all the time. This cooled them a little, and they scrambled back wet and panting.

"It would be an awful thing if one of us let go the raft," said Tom. "It's going at such a pace that it would soon leave us behind in the sea and we'd never be found again."

"Well, for goodness' sake hang on tightly then, next time we cool ourselves," said Andy. "What about something to eat?"

They opened a tin of salmon and a tin of pears, and had a good meal, though Tom longed for some bread with the salmon. It was odd sitting there eating on the bobbing raft, all by themselves in the midst of a wide heaving sea.

The day seemed endless — but at last the sun slid down the sky and the sea turned from green to purple in the twilight. "It's not so warm now," said Tom, taking

154

his jersey down from the mast and putting it on.

"Tom, see if you can have a nap for a while," said Andy. "I don't think we ought both to sleep at once. The wind might change, or a storm might blow up—you sleep now and I'll have a nap later."

Tom wrapped himself in a rug and tried to go to sleep. Andy slipped a rope round his waist and tied him to the box in the middle.

"You might roll off the raft in the middle of the night," he said with a grin. "I shouldn't like to look round and find you gone, Tom!"

Tom lay on his back and looked up at the night sky. It was a clear night, with no moon and the stars shone brightly. Andy pointed out the North Star to Tom.

"That tells me we are still going in the right direction," said Andy. "At this rate we should sight the coast we're heading for in about three or four days."

"Oh—as long as that!" said Tom in great disappointment. "I thought we'd only be a day or two, going at this pace."

"This is a raft, not a sailing-smack," said Andy. "Now go to sleep. I'll wake you if I need you for anything."

Tom slept. He dreamt he was on a swing, going up and down, up and down in the air. It was very pleasant. Then he dreamt he was being scolded by Jill for something and she suddenly threw a pail of cold water right over him! He woke with a jump and sat up.

"Did that wave wake you?" said Andy with a grin. "I thought it would. It popped its head up, saw you asleep and jumped right on you!"

Tom laughed and lay down again. He thought about Andy—what a good sort he was—always doing what he felt was best and wisest—never grumbling—always

155

willing to do the hardest job. It was a good thing Tom and the girls had had Andy to help them.

Andy awoke Tom near dawn and told him to sit up and keep watch. "The wind's still right," he said. "Watch it, Tom. You can see the North Star, can't you? I'm so sleepy I can't keep awake much longer."

Andy tied himself up safely, lay down and was asleep as his head touched the rug that made a pillow for him. Tom sat and watched the dawn coming. It was a wonderful sight. First the sky turned to silver and the sea turned to silver too. Soon a pink flush came into the eastern sky and then it changed to a blaze of gold. The sea sparkled and glinted with gold too.

Tom wished he could wake Andy up and make him see the magnificent sight. There was nothing but sea and sky, all glowing with colour. But Andy was tired and Tom sat and watched it by himself, half afraid of the strange beauty around him.

After a while Tom felt very hungry. He burrowed in the box of food to see what there was. He felt like a meal of tongue or ham. He picked out a tin of tongue and opened it. It smelt delicious.

Andy woke up after a while and shared the meat with Tom. They opened some pineapple and had that too. The juice was very pleasant. They poured water into the tin and made a kind of pineapple drink to have later on in the day.

Andy sniffed the wind, and looked at the sky. "There's a change coming," he said. "I do hope we shan't be blown out of our way. We were getting on so well!"

The sea was rougher. Waves slopped over the deck almost every minute now. Only by sitting up on the box of food could the boys keep dry from the waist up. Once

156

or twice the raft heeled over, and Tom had to clutch the mast to keep from over-balancing.

"Blow!" said Tom. "What does the sea want to get so rough for? It's a good thing we're both good sailors or we'd be very ill."

Andy looked anxiously at the sky. "I'm afraid the wind is changing," he said. "We shall be blown right out of our way if it does. The sea is getting very rough, Tom. I think we'd both better tie ourselves firmly to the mast. It won't do for either of us to be thrown off the raft —and a big wave could easily dash one of us overboard!"

So they tied themselves to the mast, and then watched the scurrying clouds, wondering if they would suddenly slow down—and fly the other way!

XXIII

A WONDERFUL SURPRISE

Alas for Tom and Andy! The wind did change and blew
strongly the other way. Andy took down the sail hurriedly.
"We don't want to be blown back to our island!" he said.
"We must just bob along without a sail now and hope
for the best. When the wind changes again we'll put up
the sail once more."

"I wonder if the enemy has found out that we've
escaped," said Tom. "They might send a seaplane out
after us if they've found out we've gone. They'd know we
were on a raft."

"Well, the girls wouldn't give us away, that's certain,"
said Andy. "But the enemy might easily guess we'd made
a raft, if they searched the island for us and missed us
—and they could send out a seaplane or two to hunt the
seas for us. We're a good way from the island now—but
a seaplane could easily find us."

"I hope one doesn't," said Tom. "Isn't this wind
hateful, Andy? It just won't stop! It's wasting all our
time."

The wind blew cold. The sun was behind the clouds.
Big waves slapped around the raft and seemed really
spiteful. "Almost as if they want to snatch us off," said
Tom, tightening the rope that tied him safely to the mast.
He shivered. There was no shelter at all on the open
raft, and no way of getting warm or dry now that the
sun was not to be seen.

"Do a few arm exercises, Tom," said Andy. "That will

get you a bit warmer!" The boys swung their arms and slapped themselves.

The waves raced along and the raft raced along too — but not in the right direction, Tom was sure!

And then, towards afternoon, the wind dropped again, and the sun shone out! What a relief that was! The boys sunned themselves gladly, and were soon warm. Andy rigged the sail again. "We'll get the wind we want this evening," he said. "We'll be ready for it."

Sure enough, as the sun slid down the western sky, the wind got up again — and this time it was blowing from the right quarter! Andy was delighted.

The sail flapped and the little raft raced along nobly. "I think the wind's set in properly now," said Andy, pleased. "If only it holds for another couple of days we may be home — or, at any rate, see a ship we can hail."

The wind became stiffer as the evening drew on. The sun was just about to slip over the sky-line when Andy sat up straight and looked alarmed.

"Can you hear a noise?" he asked Tom.

"Plenty," said Tom. "The wind and the waves and the sail!"

"No — not that sort of noise," said Andy. "A noise like — a seaplane!"

Tom's heart almost stopped beating. Surely their escape hadn't been discovered after all! He sat and listened.

"Yes — there's a seaplane about somewhere," said Andy. "Blow! If it's really hunting for us it will be sure to find us. Just as we've got away so nicely, too — and the wind helping us again, and all!"

Tom went pale, and looked up at the sky anxiously. Both boys could now hear the hum of the engines quite clearly.

And then the seaplane appeared, flying fairly low and quite slowly. It was plain that it was hunting the seas for something.

"Can we do anything, Andy?" said Tom.

"We had better jump into the water, hold on to the raft, and hope maybe the seaplane will think there's no one on it," said Andy. "Only our heads will show beside the raft—they might not notice them. Come on, quick!"

The boys slid into the water over the side of the raft. They hung there with their hands, only their heads showing. They waited anxiously.

The great seaplane came zooming overhead, very close to the water. It had seen the raft and was coming to examine it more closely. How the boys hoped that when the raft was seen to be empty the seaplane would fly off!

The plane flew over the raft. It circled round and came back again, flying once more over the raft. It circled round again and the boys hoped it would now fly off. But once more it flew over the raft—and then, to the boys' great dismay, it skimmed over the water and landed there, not very far off.

"It's no good, Tom. We're discovered," said Andy. "We may as well climb back on to the raft. Look—they're letting down a boat."

The boys climbed back on to the raft, angry and disappointed. And then Tom gave such a tremendous yell that Andy nearly fell overboard with fright.

"Andy! ANDY! Look at the sign on the seaplane! It's British! It's BRITISH!"

Andy looked—and sure enough there was the well-known mark that all British machines wear! And then such a change came over the boys. Instead of sitting there sullen and angry, they went completely mad. They stood up and danced on that rocking raft! They yelled, they waved, they stamped! And, as you can imagine, Tom lost his balance and fell right into the water.

Andy pulled him in, gasping and spluttering. "Oh, Andy, it's a British seaplane—not the enemy. Golly! Suppose it had flown off and not come down to examine the raft!" And then Tom went mad again and shouted for joy.

The boat from the seaplane came nearer. It had two men in it, and they hailed the boys.

"Ahoy there! Where are you from?"

"Ahoy there!" yelled back Andy. "Ahoy there!" He was too excited to shout anything else. The boat came alongside the raft and the men pulled the two boys into it.

"Why, it's only a couple of boys," said one man. "We reckoned you might be men from a sunk ship or aeroplane. How did you get here?"

"It's a long tale to tell," said Andy. "I think I'd better tell it to the chief, if you don't mind."

"All right. The commander's in the plane," said the first man. They rowed off to the seaplane, and left the little raft bobbing about on the sea alone. Tom was quite sorry to see it go. He had got fond of it. He was sorry to think of the wasted food, too!

The boat reached the enormous seaplane. The boys were pushed up into it, and a grave-faced man turned to receive them.

And then Andy got a second shock, for Tom once more let out a yell that really scared him!

"DADDY! Oh, DADDY! It's YOU!"

The grave-faced man stared at Tom as if he couldn't believe his eyes. Then he took the boy into his arms and gave him such a bear-like hug that Tom felt as if his bones would break!

"Tom! We've been hunting for you ever since we heard you had gone off in that boat and hadn't come back!" he said. "Where are the girls—quick, tell me!"

"They're safe," said Tom. "We left them on the island. They're quite safe. Oh, Daddy—isn't this too good to be true! Daddy, this is Andy. He's been such a brick. We'd never have escaped if it hadn't been for him."

"What do you mean—*escaped*?" said Tom's father in surprise. "Escaped from what?"

"We've got a big secret to tell you," said Tom. "We've

found out something queer. You tell him, Andy."

"Well, sir," said Andy, "we got thrown off up the coast of some desolate islands where nobody lives now. The enemy are using them for their submarines and seaplanes. There are caves stored with food—and there must be stores of fuel somewhere, too."

"What!" shouted Tom's father. He called his men near and they all listened to Andy's tale. The boy told it well.

"And we were just escaping on the raft we had made when we saw you," finished Andy. "We slipped over the side of the raft to hide—but you must have seen us."

"We didn't," said Tom's father. "But we were puzzled about the empty raft and came down to examine it. Little did we think you and Andy were there! This seaplane and two others have been scouring the seas about here looking for the sailing-ship you went off in. We were afraid you might be drifting about in it, half-starving. Your poor mother has been dreadfully upset."

"Oh dear, I was afraid she would be," said Tom. "But, never mind, we're all safe, Daddy—at least, I *hope* the girls are safe!"

"They will be, very soon," said the boy's father in a grim voice. "We shall rescue them—and clean up those submarines and seaplanes in no time! How clever of the enemy to have a base just under our noses—but it won't last long now! You've done a marvellous thing, Tom and Andy!"

"I hope my father won't be very angry with me for losing his boat," said Andy. "Though we might perhaps be able to get it back from the enemy now."

"Your father won't be angry with you for anything once he sees you are safe, and hears the tale you have just told me!" said Tom's father. "Settle down now—we're going up."

"Back to the island to rescue the girls?" asked Tom eagerly. His father shook his head.

"No," he said. "They must wait, I'm afraid, till I get this news through. I'll wireless home that we've got you safe, and have got great news—but that's all. This is too important to be told to anyone but the chief himself."

With a great noise of engines, the seaplane skimmed over the water, and then rose gracefully in the air. She shot away southwards, and the boys looked out over the sea, which was now far below.

"Well, what luck to be rescued like this!" said Andy. "And oh, Tom—what a shock the enemy are going to get!"

XXIV

WHAT HAPPENED TO THE GIRLS

The two girls felt very lost and lonely when the boys went off on the raft. They climbed the cliff quickly so that they might watch the boys till they were out of sight.

They waved until the raft was a tiny speck on the sea. Then they lost sight of it. It was gone.

"I do hope Tom and Andy reach home all right," said Jill, as they made their way down the cliff to the shore again. "It would be awful if they got lost on the sea."

"Don't say things like that!" said Mary. "Let's think of something cheerful! Let's have something to eat."

But neither of them really wanted anything. They kept thinking of the two brave boys on their little raft.

"I do hope nobody comes to the island today," said Mary. "I don't feel as if I shall be able to act very well."

Nobody did come that day. The girls were left quite alone. They bathed in the sea and dried themselves in the sun. Then they bathed all over again. There really wasn't much else to do!

They missed the two boys very much, and when night came they even felt a little frightened.

"Cheer up!" said Jill, seeing Mary's long face. "We shall be all right cuddled up in the tent together! The enemy don't know the boys are gone—that's the main thing. I should think the boys are pretty safe by now—there has been a good wind blowing all day and they must have gone a long way already."

The girls lighted their little stove and put it just at

the tent-opening when night came. They liked to see the small light it gave. They boiled a kettle of water on it and sat inside the tent, drinking hot cocoa, whilst the stars came out in the sky.

As they were about to curl up and go to sleep they heard the sound of a seaplane droning overhead. It came over the island twice, and then went away.

And then, about an hour later, the girls heard the noise of the motor-boat! It grounded on the sand of the cove and the girls heard men's voices.

"Good gracious!" said Jill, sitting up in alarm. "What are they coming here at this time of night for? They will soon see the boys aren't here! Quick, Mary, get up. We'll slip out of the tent and go into the bracken. Maybe we can pretend we've been roaming over the island, and they'll think the boys are somewhere about too."

The girls left the tent and ran into the heather and bracken in the middle of the small island. The men left their boat on the beach and two of them came up to the tent.

They lifted the flap of the tent and flashed a torch inside. There was no one there, of course! One of the men called out loudly.

"Now, you children! Where are you?"

"Here!" answered Jill. She nudged Mary. "You shout too," she whispered. "Then I'll shout again, and they'll think we are all here."

"We're here!" yelled Mary valiantly, though her heart was beating hard.

"In the bracken!" shouted Jill.

"Come along down here," commanded the man. He was the one who could speak English.

"We shall have to go," said Jill. "Now don't you give

the boys away, Mary. Pretend they are about somewhere."

The girls made their way to the men, who flashed a light on them.

"Where are the boys?" demanded the man.

"Haven't you seen them?" asked Jill. "They must be about somewhere. Maybe they are in the tent. Have you looked?"

"Yes," said the man. "Now look here — what do you mean by lighting this stove out here? Are you trying to signal to anyone?"

"Good gracious! Of course not!" said Jill. "We only made some hot cocoa, that's all. Look — there are our dirty cups."

She wished she had not said this when the man looked for the cups — for he saw at once that there were only two! He looked at Jill suspiciously.

"Why did the boys not have the cocoa?" he asked.

"They weren't here when we made it," said Jill. "Why don't you go and look for them?"

The man turned out the stove, and the light flickered and went out. "Now don't you dare to show a light at nights," he said. "If I think you are signalling to anyone you will be very sorry!"

"Who could we signal to?" asked Jill. "We don't even know where we are!"

The man took no notice of her. He stood and shouted into the night. "Boys! Come here at once!"

There was no answer, of course — there couldn't be, for the boys were miles away on the sea.

"To-morrow I will come to tell those boys that when I call, they must answer," said the man in an angry voice. "I am going now — but to-morrow I come again. You will tell the boys they must be here, by the tent."

Jill and Mary said nothing. They could not tell the boys — and they wondered what would happen when the men found that they were not on the island.

The men went off in their boat again. "What a pity we lighted that stove!" said Jill. "I suppose that seaplane saw it and reported it — and they thought we were signalling to someone. How clever they must think us! I only wish we *could* signal to someone!"

Neither of the girls could imagine what the men would do when they came to find the boys the next day, and saw that they were gone. They cuddled up together and tried to go to sleep. They awoke early and got themselves some breakfast. Then they sat waiting for the men.

There was nothing else to do — it was of no use trying to hide. They must just pretend that they did not know where the boys were.

The motor-boat did not arrive until mid-day. Then two men came up to the tent, and the one who could speak English looked at the two girls.

"What about those boys?" he said. "Why are they not here?"

"I don't know," said Jill, trying to speak bravely.

"Where are they?" asked the man angrily.

"I don't know," said Jill again, quite truthfully.

"You don't know! You don't know!" said the man in disgust. "It is time you did know. Are they on this island?"

"Why don't you look and see?" said Jill. "I am sure you will not believe what I say — so you had better look."

The men glared at the plucky little girl and then went to hunt over the island. They found no one, of course, and returned looking worried.

They spoke to one another in a language that the girls could not understand. Then they went to the ruined buildings and looked around carefully. It did not take them long to see that the boys had pulled the old shack to pieces.

"So!" said the first man. "The boys tried to make a boat!"

Jill and Mary shook their heads. They were really feeling very much alarmed.

"It is a raft they made then?" asked the man. "What! You will not tell me, you naughty little girls! Then I shall order out my seaplanes and they will find those bad boys, and bring them back again. And you will all be made prisoners on another island till we take you far away to our country where you will stay for a long time."

The girls began to cry—not because they were afraid for themselves but because they did not want the seaplanes to hunt for Andy and Tom.

The men spoke quickly to one another. It was plain that they wanted to get back to the third island and tell their chief what had happened.

"We shall come back for you to-morrow," said the first man. "And maybe by that time we shall have caught the two bad boys. They will be punished, you may be sure!"

They left in their motor-boat, leaving two miserable girls behind them. "Oh, I do hope they won't catch poor Andy and Tom," wept Mary. "It's too bad! Now they will hunt all over the sea till they find them. And they'll catch us to-morrow too, and take us all away."

"Well, they just won't take *me* away!" said Jill, drying her eyes fiercely. "I shall give them a good old hunt for me! I shall go to the second island and make them hunt all over the first one and not find me! That will give them a shock! I shall hide in the food-cave!"

"So will I!" said Mary, dabbing her eyes fiercely too. "We'll wait till the tide goes down and then we'll clamber over the rocks!"

So when the tide was low that day the two girls clambered hurriedly over the line of rocks that led from one island to the next, and came to the sandy beach. Not far off was the entrance to the cave that led up to the Round Cave.

"Nobody has seen us," said Mary, as they ran up to the cave. "We'll hide here and make the enemy think *we've* escaped from the island too! Perhaps they will be so busy looking for us that they will forget about the boys."

"I don't think they'll forget Andy and Tom," said Jill, making her way up the passage to the Round Cave. "I am sure that seaplanes are out looking for them already. I have heard three or four leaving the third island. Look, Mary—this chest is almost empty. Let's take out the tins and things that are left and get inside. We can shut the lid down on us if we hear anyone coming."

The girls got the chest ready, and then amused themselves by trying to find the funnel opening that led from the cave to the surface of the cliff above. But they could not find it.

"I wonder if it's night yet," said Mary, for it was impossible to tell in the dark cave. The girls had Andy's torch, for no daylight came into the cave at all. They crept to the shore-cave to see. Yes—it was twilight outside. Night would soon fall.

"I vote we make a nice soft bed in the sandy floor,"

said Jill. "We can cover ourselves with those empty sacks. And in the morning we'll peep out and see if we can see anything!"

So they made sandy beds and threw the sacks over themselves. They fell fast asleep and did not wake till morning.

And then, when they went to peep out of the shore-cave, they had a great surprise! Coming gracefully down to the smooth water was an enormous seaplane, droning like a great bumble-bee.

"It's coming to get us!" squealed Mary in fright, and the two girls scuttled back into the Round Cave!

XXV

RETURN TO THE ISLANDS

If only the girls had stopped to look carefully at that seaplane, they would have noticed that it bore the signs of their *own* country! It was the very same seaplane that had rescued Tom and Andy! It had flown to headquarters, had made its report, and had handed Tom's camera in.

As soon as the pictures had been developed, and the seaplane and submarine photographs had come out clearly, there was great excitement.

Tom and Andy had been questioned closely. They told their story clearly and well, and the men who listened to them were amazed at the adventures the four children had been through.

"Well, you have stumbled on an astonishing secret," said one man who had been listening. "We are proud of you! Now we shall be able to spring a real surprise on our enemy, and clean up all the submarines and seaplanes that have been worrying our shipping for some time. We did not know they had a base so near us. No wonder they have been able to do such damage!"

"Please, sir, what about my sisters?" asked Tom anxiously. "Will you get them away before you do anything?"

The men laughed heartily. "Of course!" said one. "That will be our first job. You don't really suppose we should forget those two plucky little girls, do you? Oh no—we shall send your father's seaplane to rescue them—and after that—oho! A big surprise will come to those islands!"

The boys grinned. "May we see the surprise, sir?" asked Andy.

"No," said the man. "It will be a bit too noisy." He turned to Tom's father and gave him a few quick orders.

"Come along," said the boy's father. "You and Andy must come with me to the islands so that you may tell me quickly where the girls are. We have to get them off before we attack the enemy—and I'd like to do it as quickly as possible before anyone knows we've discovered their secret!"

The boys were thrilled! To go off in that wonderful seaplane again—to the islands! And to rescue the two girls under the very noses of the enemy! What fun!

They all went aboard the great seaplane. They rowed out to it in a little boat and climbed up the ladder over the side, and into the plane. A few quick orders, and the great engines were started up.

R-r-r-r-r! R-r-r-r-r-r! R-r-r-r-r-r-r-r! The seaplane skimmed over the water for a little while and then rose from the surface as gracefully as a gull. It soared up and round, and then flew in a straight line towards the far-off islands.

The boys were trembling with excitement and joy. They had had many adventures, but this last one, the rescue of the girls, was the finest of the lot! They looked out over the sea, watching for the first sign of the islands they now knew so well.

"As soon as we sight the islands, we are going cautiously," said Tom's father. "We don't want to warn the enemy if we can help it! You say there is a good landing-place off the shore of the second island, Andy.

Well, you must guide us there when the islands come in sight, and we'll land on the water. Then you and Tom and a couple of men can get to the first island and take off the girls. Then off we'll go again and give the signal for the warships to go and surprise the enemy!"

"Warships!" cried the boys. "I say! What a shock for the enemy!"

"It's a shock they deserve," said Tom's father grimly. "We are sending three warships and some aeroplanes to deal with the submarines and seaplanes. So, you see, we want to get the girls off as quickly as possible."

"Oh, golly, wouldn't I like to join the fight!" groaned Andy. "Oh, couldn't I, sir?"

"No," said Tom's father. But he smiled at the eager boy and clapped him on the shoulder. "You're a good lad, Andy," he said, "and I'm glad that my three children had your help in their amazing adventures!"

Andy went red with pleasure. He thought Tom's father was a fine man, dressed in his grand uniform. He wondered what his own father would say when he heard all their adventures—and in his secret mind he felt a little uncomfortable because his father would have to hear the news that his fishing-boat had been lost.

The boys kept a watch for the islands—and as soon as they caught sight of them, lying flat in the sea, they both shouted loudly:

"There they are!"

"The islands, the islands!"

"Which is the one the girls are on?" asked Tom's father eagerly. Tom showed him.

"The first one," he said. "And the next one is where the food-cave is, and the third one is where the submarines are. I don't know anything about the other islands

174

further off. We didn't have time to explore those."

"Well, *we* shall," said the boy's father, in a grim tone. "Now, Tom, we are almost on the coast of the second island. Is that the smooth bit of water we can land on, just down there?"

"Yes!" cried both boys, as they saw the flat stretch of water that lay between the reef of rocks and the cave-beach. The seaplane circled round and flew down gracefully. She skimmed the water a little, like a swallow, and then came to rest, bobbing up and down as she lay there.

"The tide is a bit too deep over the rocks that lead to the first island," said Tom in disappointment. "We can't climb over them to rescue the girls yet."

"We'll take a boat, then," said his father. "Are those the caves you hid in, Tom?"

"Yes—that one just there is the one that leads to the food-cave," said Tom. "Like to see it, Daddy? You might find something of importance there, perhaps."

"Yes—we might as well have a look," said the boy's father. So a boat shot off from the seaplane carrying the two boys, Tom's father, and two men. They landed on the beach and went towards the cave.

The girls were hiding inside the chest when they heard footsteps coming up the passage-way that led from the shore-cave to the Round Cave. They lay there trembling, wondering when they were going to be discovered.

Tom led his father into the cave. "Look!" he said, "do you see all these boxes and chests, Daddy? They are absolutely *full* of food of all sorts. I can tell you it came in handy when we were so hungry. At first I kept a list of the things we took, thinking that we would pay for them when we discovered the owner, but——"

Tom stopped. A queer noise was coming from a big chest near by. He stared in surprise.

"What's that noise?" said Tom's father at once.

"I don't know," said Tom. "Listen!"

It was the girls inside the chest, of course! They had heard Tom's voice, and they were quite mad with joy and excitement—but they couldn't lift up the lid of the chest which they had carefully shut down over themselves! It had got so tightly fastened that they could not push it up, and the two girls were shouting and banging on the lid to make themselves heard.

"There's something in that chest," said Tom in a trembling voice. "Is it the enemy playing a trick?"

"We'll soon see," said his father, in a fierce voice. He rapped out an order to the two men with him, and they went over to the chest. They ripped off the lid—and everyone stood ready to fight the enemy.

But it was two small, excited, and most untidy little girls who rose up from the chest, shouting loudly:

"Tom! Andy! It's us! We hid here because we thought you were the enemy!"

Their father picked them out of the chest and hugged them. They were as surprised as he was! They simply couldn't believe their eyes!

"Daddy! It's you! However did you get here? Oh, Tom! Andy! You've come to rescue us just in time. Oh, what a good thing you came to the cave!"

"Why are you here?" asked the boys.

Jill and Mary told their tale, their words tumbling over one another. When their father heard that the enemy guessed that the boys had left on a raft, he hustled them all out of the cave very quickly.

"We'll get back to our plane," he said. "We shall get into a spot of trouble if the enemy see us here. If they really think the boys have gone to tell their secret they will be watching for us—though not expecting us quite so soon. Come along!"

They all rowed off to the seaplane. The girls were thrilled to get inside it, and even more excited when it rose into the air and left the sea far below.

"Good-bye, little islands," said Jill, watching them get smaller and smaller as the plane left them behind. "We've had lots of adventures on you—but I'm very glad to leave you, all the same!"

The boys were looking down as the plane flew swiftly along. Suddenly Tom gave a shout.

"Warships! Look! Steaming below us at top speed! Are they going to the islands?"

"They are," said his father. "There will be quite a lot of noise round about your islands very soon! And, look—here are aeroplanes, too, to help the warships."

A flight of aeroplanes flew near the seaplane. The children felt tremendously excited. What a pity they had left before the fun began!

"And now, home we go to your mother," said the children's father, "and to Andy's father. Both will be so very glad to have you back again."

"But what will my father say about his lost fishing-boat?" wondered poor Andy. "Whatever *will* he say?"

XXVI

THE END OF THE ADVENTURES

The seaplane flew over the water, and at last came to the shores of the little fishing-village where Andy lived, and the other three children had been staying. It glided down to the water, and rested there, its great wings spread out beside it.

The little beach was soon crowded with people — fishermen and their wives, children, visitors — all shouting and cheering. The news had gone round that the four missing children had been found!

A boat set off to fetch the children from the plane. It was rowed by Andy's father! How Andy shouted to see him!

"Dad! We're back again!"

The bearded man in the boat smiled and waved. He had been terribly worried about Andy and the children — but now his heart was glad. They were safe!

The children tumbled into the boat, all talking at once. Andy's father patted his boy on the shoulder and smiled at him out of eyes as blue as Andy's. Neither of them said very much, but their hands pressed one another joyfully. Tom's father came with them. He had two days' leave and was going to spend it with his wife and children.

The people on the beach cheered and shouted. The little boat grounded and was pulled up the shore by willing hands. Everyone wanted to shake hands and say how glad they were to see the children back. And then the children saw their mother! They rushed to her and hugged her like bears, shouting and laughing.

"Now, now, give me a look in," said their father, smiling, and the whole family went up the beach together. Andy went off with his father. He had no mother, so he thought twice as much of his father.

What a talking and chattering there was that evening! The children's mother made them all strip off their dirty clothes and have a good bath before they did anything.

"I don't know you when you look so dreadfully dirty!" she said. "Put on clean clothes, for goodness' sake!"

Soon they were all clean and dressed in other clothes. It felt nice to be tidy and fresh again. They hung round their mother and tried to tell her all their adventures at once.

"Andy was marvellous," said Tom. "We could never have done what we did if it hadn't been for him. The girls were pretty brave too — I was proud of them."

"And old Tom didn't do so badly — except that he left his precious camera behind and got us all into a fix!" said Jill. "He was as brave as could be."

"Well, I'm proud of you all," said their mother, hugging them. "But oh, I was so awfully worried when you didn't come back. I sent a message to your father and he came in his seaplane and hunted for you for days. He wouldn't give up hunting — and it's a good thing he didn't, for he found you just in time! You and Andy would never, never have got home on that little raft, you know, Tom."

"Wouldn't we?" said Tom, surprised. "I thought we really might."

"I don't think Andy thought there was much hope," said the children's father, "but he knew it was your only chance — and he knew, besides, that it was his duty to tell someone the great secret you had discovered. It means a lot to our country to know the secret of those desolate little islands."

There was a dull booming sound as the children's father finished speaking. Tom looked at his father.

"Is that guns?" he asked.

"Yes. It will be the end of those hateful submarines," said his father gravely. "There will be no more of our ships sunk without warning by *that* nest of submarines! And I rather think that our aeroplanes will drive off any seaplanes round about those islands—those that are not destroyed will fly to their own country in fear! They are no match for our pilots!"

The children were silent as they listened to the guns booming far away again. They were all imagining the islands echoing to the terrific sound of gun-fire. Mary began to cry.

Her father put his arm round her. "Yes, Mary," he said, "it is something to cry about, to think that we have to fight so much evil and wickedness. It is right against wrong and we have to be strong and courageous when we fight such a powerful and evil enemy as ours. But dry your eyes—you are on the right side and that is something to be proud of!"

Andy came tearing up to the cottage. "I say!" he yelled. "Do you hear the guns? I guess they are waking up the islands! What a shock for the enemy!"

"Andy, was your father angry about his fishing-boat being lost?" asked Tom, who knew how much Andy was dreading what his father might say about that.

"He hasn't said a word about it," said Andy. "Not a word. He's been fine about it. We're going to fish with my uncle, now that we've lost our own boat. Maybe one day we'll save enough money to get a boat again."

"I wouldn't worry about that, if I were you," said Tom's father unexpectedly. "I rather think there is a surprise coming for you to-morrow!"

"Oh, what?" cried all the children, and Andy stared at Tom's father in surprise.

"Wait and see," was the answer. So they had to wait —and the next day the surprise arrived!

Andy saw it first. He was on the beach, mending nets, and the other children were helping him. Andy happened to look up—and he saw a fishing-boat rounding the corner of the cliff

"Hallo!" said Andy. "Whose boat is that? I haven't seen it before! My word, what a smart one! Look at its red sail!"

The children stood up and watched the little fishing-boat drawing in to shore. It was a real beauty, fresh with new paint, and with its red sail billowing out in the breeze.

It came in to the beach and a man jumped out. He saw the children and hailed them. "Hie, give a hand here!"

They ran to help. "Whose boat is this?" asked Tom.

"I've got to find the owner," said the man. "It's for the boy whose name has been given to the boat."

The children looked at the name on the boat. There, painted boldly, was Andy's own name—ANDY!

"*Andy!* The boat is called *Andy!*" squealed Jill. "Oh, Andy, does that mean it's for you?"

Andy stared at the boatman in astonishment and joy. "It *can't* be for me!" he said.

"Well, if you're Andy, it's yours," said the boatman. "I understand that it's a little reward from the Government

182

of our country for good services; wasn't it you who discovered the secret of those islands, and lost your own boat in doing so?"

"Golly!" said Andy, and could say no more. He stood and stared at the lovely boat in delight and pride. It was the finest in the bay. It was beautiful all over. Never, never could Andy ever have saved enough money to buy a boat like this!

The other three children were full of joy. They had been so sorry for Andy when his boat had been lost, for they knew that he and his father got their living from fishing. And now Andy had a much better boat—they couldn't keep back their joy. They danced and shouted and clapped Andy on the back till the boy almost fell over.

"You shall share the boat with me," said Andy, suddenly finding his tongue again. "It shall belong to all of us!"

"Well, we have to go back to school again soon," said Tom, rather sadly. "But we're to come here for holidays always, Andy—so we can share it then. Can't we go out in it now?"

Many people had come down to the beach to look at the fine new fishing-boat. Andy's father and uncle came running down—and when they heard the news they could not believe their ears!

"It's called *Andy*," said Tom proudly. "Isn't it a fine boat? It's because Andy was so brave and helped his country such a lot. And he's going to share it with us when we come here for our holidays."

Andy's father got into the boat and looked at it carefully. His blue eyes gleamed with joy. "Ah, Andy lad," he said, "this is a wonderful boat. We'll go out on the tide this evening, and do a wee bit of fishing together! And you must write to the Government to thank them for their bonny present! It's most generous of them!"

Andy was not a good writer, so Tom wrote the letter for him and posted it. And then Andy, his father, and the three children all got into the fishing-boat that evening to make the first trip together.

The red sail billowed out against the sky, as the evening breeze filled it. Like a sea-bird the little boat bobbed gracefully on the water — and then raced away on the tide. The *Andy* was away on her first trip!

"Now don't get lost on any more adventures!" shouted the children's father, who had come down to the beach to watch. "Just go fishing now — and bring me back something for breakfast! I don't want submarines and seaplanes this time!"

Everyone laughed. The sail flapped happily, and the boat sped on like a live thing towards the fishing-grounds.

"She feels a good boat, bonny and brave!" said Andy's father.

"The *Andy* is like her master then!" cried Tom. "For he's just the same. Good luck to the *Andy*, so bonny and brave — and good luck to you too, Andy!"

And there we will leave them all, scudding along in the *Andy* — and we'll say the same — good luck to you, Andy, and your red-sailed boat! Good luck!